Setting the Lawn on Fire

Setting the Lawn on Fire

A Novel

Mack Friedman

Terrace Books
A trade imprint of the University of Wisconsin Press

Terrace Books
A trade imprint of the University of Wisconsin Press
1930 Monroe Street, 3rd Floor
Madison, Wisconsin 53711-2059

www.wisc.edu/wisconsinpress/

3 Henrietta Street
London WC2E 8LU, England

3   5   4   2

Printed in the United States of America

Library of Congress Cataloging-in-Publication Data

Friedman, Mack.
Setting the lawn on fire : a novel / Mack Friedman.
    p.   cm.
ISBN 0-299-21340-4 (cloth: alk. paper)
1. Jewish youth—Fiction.   2. Milwaukee (Wis.)—Fiction.
3. Americans—Mexico—Fiction.   4. Gay youth—Fiction.
5. Young men—Fiction.   I. Title.
    PS3606.R566S48   2005
    813'.6—dc22   2005005441

ISBN 0-299-21344-7 (pbk.: alk. paper)

An earlier version of "The Salmon Capital of the World" was originally published in *Wonderlands: Good Gay Travel Writing,* ed. Raphael Kadushin (Madison: University of Wisconsin Press, 2004). An earlier version of "Kerosene," called "Setting the Lawn on Fire," was originally published in *Barnstorm: Contemporary Wisconsin Fiction,* ed. Raphael Kadushin (Madison: University of Wisconsin Press, 2005). Reprinted by permission of the publisher. An earlier version of "Love Maps" was originally published in *Obsessed,* ed. Michael Lowenthal (NY: Plume, 1999). Reprinted by permission of the author.

Terrace Books, a trade imprint of the University of Wisconsin Press,
takes its name from the Memorial Union Terrace, located at
the University of Wisconsin–Madison. Since its inception in 1907,
the Wisconsin Union has provided a venue for students, faculty, staff,
and alumni to debate art, music, politics, and the issues of the day.
It is a place where theater, music, drama, literature, dance, outdoor activities,
and major speakers are made available to the campus and the community.
To learn more about the Union, visit www.union.wisc.edu.

FOR KATE

The median age of pubescence for girls has been found to be thirteen years and nine months in New York and Chicago.

Vladimir Nabokov, *Lolita*

Contents

Acknowledgments

Many thanks to my wonderful editor, Raphael Kadushin, whose humor, patience, and sound advice guided and sustained this writing. Thanks also to Sue Breckenridge for her careful and incisive copyedits, and to Sheila Moermond, Colin Fleming, and everyone at the University of Wisconsin Press who helped during this project, for their enthusiastic and seamless teamwork. I would also like to acknowledge the following people for their insight and interest: Robin Arnold, Bruce Benderson, Sharon Bernstein, Brian Broome, Jerome Crooks, Clay Eccard, Lesley Foster, Brian Funk, Alison Garber, Shira Hassan, Justin Honard, Michelle Lane, J. T. LeRoy, Michael Lowenthal, P. K. McBee, Valerie Miner, el roy red, Beth Steidle, Christopher Ungerer, Adrienne Walnoha, and Thomas Waugh. Finally, inexpressible gratitude to my family, especially my parents, neither dead nor absent, for their love and support.

Setting the Lawn on Fire

Kerosene

It's the first day of school, third grade. Where are you? Are you there? Do you remember the leaves starting to change, the breeze cooling hips under shorts? Were you looking down at your new shoes? I looked up on my way to the bus, saw a boy.

And that's really my story. A nine-year-old stranger. Saucony sneakers, gold-striped foam soles. Concrete squares, an arching blue dawn, sunlit rooftops. The shadow I wound up in, underneath the U-Frame-It. Teeth as white as sheets. A feeling, as he hugged me, of a dream. Not a dream I had slept through, but a living reverie, a dream that followed me, the way people are haunted by brilliance. Or a physical imprinting, a makers' mark pressed into the quicksand of a sidewalk—Milwaukee WI 1979—before it slowly turns hard and impenetrable.

Green *Journal* box, green light, WALK in pale letters. I ran to him. He turned his head and grinned.

"Are you going to Fighting Bob LaFollette Elementary?" he asked.

3

"Yes," I said, and was next to him, looking up at his face, where the sky bored two holes to see through.

"Me too!" he said. "I'm in fourth grade." He threw himself at me. We hugged so hard my backpack fell off my shoulders.

Cal was my guide. I barely noticed my new school. I couldn't wait for recess, when I'd see him again. He was Cal with a capital C. He lived around the corner. We were friends.

The boulevard where I grew up slid gently down the block, perfect for football. We played with his little brother, Ronnie, who was in second grade. One summer morning I cut across the grass and slammed forehead-first into a concrete lamppost. It knocked me out just as I registered its flat enormity. Cal caressed me back into consciousness, as if willing the goose egg that swelled on my forehead to hatch. He picked a dead dandelion and blew off its head so the spores drifted under my nostrils. Ronnie ran for my dad, who came out with ice. Of this there remains scar tissue, a mass of my cranium shaped like a tennis ball's extrusion into air when it's floating on the surface of a pool.

In the summers we all took tennis and swim lessons. At first I was jealous, but I learned to tolerate Ronnie's tagging along. Once we showered near a man who was shaving his crotch. We were entranced enough to make fun of him walking home. I know I thought about pubic hair on me or on Cal, but the idea seemed so removed from what was there that I quickly got distracted.

I knew what was there by watching him change now and then. When he combed his straight blond hair at the sinks, I'd stay at the lockers and survey his white Hanes for shit stains. One day Ronnie couldn't come, dentist or something. Cal and I walked back alone from the pool, four blocks up Locust from the riverside. It was in July, around our birthdays. He put his arm around me. His hair was slicked back, drying in the sun, like in some Don Henley song. In the space of a pop tune, traffic receded into scenery, Cal's hand on my shoulder. I'd gone through the wardrobe and made it to Narnia. He loved me right then.

Kerosene

That fall, the nightmares started. Alone in a forest, chased by bears, in a spiral of eight-fingered oak leaves and maple pod seeds. This dream recurred through the winter and most of the spring. Then, wandering naked, night after night, onto the stage in the school cafetorium. Standing, staring out. You have to confront your fears.

I got scared my first sleepover at his house and had to go home around 11. Our next try, Cal kissed me in his upper bunk while Ronnie slept below us. It worked. I stayed the night. When they got cable TV he'd call and we'd fall asleep to 3-D horror films on the pullout in the family room. We woke up to lawnmowers, Michael Jackson, blankets over bare chests, his red, mine blue; my arm around him, its sleepy tingle pinned under his weight. His upper lip was dewy and smelled like fresh-cut grass. If they say why, tell them that it's human nature.

Once, in a late-August lightning storm, while my parents tracked the crisscrossing electricity from the back porch, we snuck into their closet and pushed the bras, hanging like curtains, from our faces. We kissed once, fast, sweet, and the breeze from the bedroom window smacked the door shut like thunder.

Last kiss: in his bunk bed, in a blizzard. We'd walked in the street to the bus stop, digging our sticks deep into sidewalk snowbanks, carving three parallel tracks. Boys do things like that in fairy tales so they won't get lost, but it almost never works. We stood in the spindrift for forty-five minutes until we realized the bus wasn't coming. Cars fumed around us, graying the salty street. On the way back to their house, we saw that new snow had already covered our tracks. This being Wisconsin, all of our parents had made it to work. Naturally, Cal, Ronnie, and I were soon running around the bedroom they shared, stark naked, yelling, "We're playing hooky!"

We caught our breath and peeked out the small, shuttered window, pressed against each other's cheeks. The snow was letting up, its violent spirals petering into jagged, gentle flakes, white butterflies fluttering down. When the last one had fallen, Cal sat down on Ronnie's bed, the lower bunk.

"One of us has to be the girl," he said to me. His lips drew back. He reclined on Ronnie's sheets. I sat next to him, facing him, mouth tingling expectantly like when my mother squeezed lemons for lemonade. Ronnie stared, his back against the wall.

"What do you mean?" I asked. Edging so slightly away.

"One of us has to be the girl. Be Jenny. Otherwise, we're just two fags kissing." And then he laughed. It seemed so out of place. He wasn't sarcastic, characteristically. But he couldn't be serious.

"Okay," I agreed. "I'll be Jenny, but we have to switch later." I knew he wouldn't, but so what.

Cal nodded, bent forward, nudged his face back into mine.

What he meant didn't sink in until much later, after we had played the bowling alley/restaurant game with plastic pins and a Nerf ball one last time. It didn't stick until long after we'd framed and clicked each other's dicks, hands shaped squarely into cameras.

What Cal said didn't hit until I was twelve, crammed into the way-back. Mom was driving me, and some of my friends, to a birthday party for a kid named Dmitri.

One boy said, "Mike P. is gonna be there."

"Mike Pee," said another boy, pretending to urinate, "is a fag."

"You boys are too young to know that about yourselves," said my mom.

I'm not, I wanted to say, *too young,* and didn't. I stared through the parallel defroster wires at the hash marks sluicing endlessly away, turning from clear into blur.

That night Dmitri's dad gave me a facial massage that felt as good as Cal's hand over my shoulder blades.

You don't have to stop, I whispered, *there,* but he didn't hear. Party boys danced in a circle as Dmitri's new Hall & Oates crested: *Because your kiss is what I miss when I turn off the lights.*

I guess in time Cal felt embarrassed. He skimmed away like a water bug, swimming butterfly strokes that I couldn't catch up with.

At practice I would glide in his contrail, stroke too close, choke in his wake. Water Safety seemed like a perfect excuse to perfect mouth-to-mouth. Instead, we tag-teamed an inflatable doll on the slippery pool deck. I nicknamed her Jenny; but when I kissed her, I pretended I was saving Cal's life.

Still, after swimming, he'd hang from my jungle gym, him and Ronnie peeing in bushes like bonobo monkeys. One blue summer day, when the breeze from the West was sweetly fervid, like corn-fields and cowshit and brewery steam, I squatted in the wood chips and watched them climb our red-white-and-blue aluminum sticks. I threw bark shavings into the grass and imagined them splintered by my father's new gas mower. On the crooked plastic swing next to the clubhouse/outhouse, I felt more certain with every creaking return that when their mom realized I was a fag and a very bad influence she wouldn't let me play with them anymore.

My dad got me a magic-trick box for my twelfth birthday, that July. It was a cheap kit, with weighted dice and invisible rope and cubist trinkets. We mastered this wizardry in two afternoons. The book that came with it, though, gave us some ideas. On its cover was a magician juggling flaming torches in the park. We started with ten-nis balls, two hours a day. Ronnie could never get the hang of it, so he was our audience. By August, we'd learned how to juggle Cal's plastic bowling pins, even passing one between us. We only dropped them once in awhile, or that's what we thought. We figured we were ready for more. I'm not even sure whose idea it was. We just followed the instructions. I collected three thick branches from the park the morning after a bad storm. Cal found some rags and wound them around the sticks, bundling them at the end with rubber bands. We dipped our kindling through the hole of the kerosene can in the ga-rage, soaked the cloth through. Ronnie brought out a box of long, red-tipped matches from my kitchen and a pail of water. Then we set the lawn on fire. It all happened so fast. The flames were out of con-trol, like Mom's hair. The neighbors called the fire department, but my dad unscrewed the sprinklers and managed to hose it all down.

In the fall when I went into eighth grade, I'd stand over my charred yard at the attic window, watch Cal and Ronnie play catch in their own fenced-off square, and try to make my phone ring. But what magic I'd learned from being Cal's assistant was useless in my hands. He ducked under the curtains in the middle of the show and left me sawed in two.

Our last date happened because Mom forced me to call him and drove us to *Dirty Dancing*. She was tired of my moping or sensed I was heartbroken. Suspecting it was a big conspiracy to show me a good time, I felt humiliated. I never called him again. I figured Cal's new trip was not a vacation. He'd never come back. Now I know I was right.

All over Wisconsin are kettles and moraines, molded by glaciers. Sometimes you can even find petrified stone.

Preserved in an icefall, life passed right by me. I fell in love with the autistic kid on *St. Elsewhere*. I thought I was enough for myself. I'd look in the glass day after day to make sure I was still there. My skin cracked from all the showers I took to get warmer. I just felt the same numbing cold all the time. In the resorts on the Upper Peninsula the snow is sometimes so frigid, skiers get stuck on the summits because their skis can't create enough friction to glide them downhill.

What's unbecoming about being stuck is just that: you cannot become. If I didn't know what I was becoming, it was because I didn't think I was. I had a sense of it, maybe, staring at my friends, but my point of view was limited: skin-deep, and they always had clothes on. The only kid I'd strip for was the one the mirror showed. I wasn't sure what was real—myself, or my reflection? There was no way for me to see my face without distortion. The closest I came was closing one eye so I could see my nose, but that was blurry and too close, out of perspective. It reminded me of filmstrips. I convinced myself the image was a counterpart: a flash of pink in my friends' retinas, a flash of pink in mine.

And so I made a friend.

Kerosene

I was thirteen then.

In colored pencil, I sketched friends in my grandfather's house, on the slim, madras couch in the den. Faces upon faces. My old friend Cal was with someone else. The latest face was cool; she wore a jean jacket, no jelly bracelets. She looked like she had staying power.

When my parents were gone, my new friend came to visit. The oval, metal-frilled frame in the downstairs bathroom showed only the top of his head: wavy brown hair, narrow, lively brown eyes. The medicine-cabinet mirror in my bathroom was rectangular but curved on top like the Liberty Bell. I saw every imperfection in the glass: the big nose with a sunburn line across the tip, chin pimple growing like a witch's wart, a kid's dumb veneer. The uncertain, anxious grin.

In the laundry room mirror I focused on my body. I'd stand next to the washer and strip, fixating on my lack of pubic hair, as though that were all that separated me from the world. I couldn't control this any more than my desire. I was repulsed and entranced to see myself as such a child. In my parents' bathroom, between opposing green walls, I reflected a leaf from one mirror onto another and saw my pale ass, undistinguished. I flexed my butt muscles and all the laws changed, like levitation. I kissed the fogging glass I had tilted, leaving my imprint. I fingered the words *I love you* over my lips in the glass, and then swabbed it all over with my hand.

At this mirror's lower counterpart, I learned I could push my penis back into my body with ease. When it was hot out, and humid, it would stay there, retracted, a negative integer. The veins under my belly button were blue below translucent skin, like the invisible man in science class. When I looked over my shoulder, my ass gleamed like moonlight.

I took long hot showers.

In seventh grade Spanish I would imagine all my classmates— black white mexican hmong japanese american, skinheaded and dyed, fat fit or skinny, big-tittied and flat—frozen at their desks, zippery parachute pants in sloppy piles for me to examine: leather cotton nylon poly fleshy bony skin like mine. It was a crash scene and

9

they were unconscious. I would have just enough time to attend to them all.

That spring, on the class trip to DC, my camera froze friends' asses under cherry blossoms. I liked it when schoolmates wore sweatpants. There was a swimming pool at the hotel. My friend Todd, his bowl-cut and rat-tail a permanent beaver hat, got naked changing into his Speedo. I saw him through the mirror in his hotel room, the eyes in the back of my head. They flickered over Todd's slight body, small penis curving over big balls like a banana split. His pubic hairs were chocolate sprinkles. I looked away, embarrassed for him in the Speedo: no one shows that much skin. Maybe I was the only one who noticed enough to care.

Stranger Danger pep rallies taught me that men could find me appealing. My gym teacher watched me bounce out of hot showers. It wasn't something that got to me, just subtle, unnamable, funny, and awkward. At first, I took in only its barest suggestions. We read Greek myths in social studies, but the legends were censored. This way, I could not identify as Narcissus, Pericles, or Ganymede. I was Icarus, led by my father out of the maze, only to burn to the ground when the sun licked my wings.

That summer, Mom and I went to New York to visit my great-aunt Joan. She was eighty-three years old, quick and fierce as a goose, and she called me Shlommy, my dad's boyhood nickname. Once when I was eight, and a flower-thrower at a family wedding, my dad gave me a plastic glass of champagne. I drank it all in one big swig in my grandfather's bathroom, like it was a cup of Tab. Then I put on some lipstick from a travel case that had to be Joan's: it was the brightest, pinkest color around. My mother asked, horrified, if I'd been putting on makeup. "Nadia, darling, he's just been kissed by so many of us," Joanie had covered for me, with a wink and a kiss. Now, at thirteen, I fought the desire to fly away naked down Columbus Avenue.

Like exotic lovers, Trocadero and Charivari opened their rooms to prepubescent afternoons. The slick men in Barneys and the guys straight from *GQ* at the sidewalk cafes. Later that summer, new wisps consumed me. I spent the family trip to California in front of mirrors in hotel bathrooms, charting each strange brown hair extruding from white skin. My dad ran mousse through my waves, roughshod. My dad's friend fired buckshot with us in his sprawling backyard, piercing warm cans of Old Milwaukee. "It's the best use for your worst beer," Tony told me, a beefy arm around my waist. "Here, hold it with both hands." He designed weapons for a living. I missed every time, but Tony made them explode against a rock barrier. Foam dribbled like tears down the sandy cliff face and into his man-made creek.

My dad's friend's daughter and her friend took me to a dance club in Santa Barbara one summer night. It was muggy and smelled like plants drinking. They had to drag me away from the Frogger arcade when "People Are People" came on. I was in *depeche mode* but my body moved slowly. I got an erection in the Pacific Ocean in my Ocean Pacific swimsuit. No one noticed. Later, I showed the boy in the mirror. He kept it to himself.

One day I got lost at Magic Mountain. The last time I was in California, I'd been eight years old. At that age I was in love with Cal. Now I wished I could touch my reflection, but I only resorbed it. Mirrors are imperfect conduits to other dimensions. Fenced inside the Lost Kids section (don't feed the animals), I hoped some nice man would kidnap me. Instead, my entourage found me and didn't. They didn't know how lost I was. I couldn't tell them. I did not know myself.

Orange Crush

Jeremy hisses through his chew.

"You going to stage crew tonight?"

The bear on his Kodiak tin peers through threadbare tan cords. We're in stage crew for *The Velveteen Rabbit* and the talent show's coming up. Last hour in Music we set up stage time with the teacher for our heavy metal cover band, The Impostors. Jer's our lead lip-syncher. I play one of the air guitars.

"Sure, why not." I poke his right arm, the skinny white part by his t-sleeve, with my pencil point. It's fourth-hour Spanish. He sits in front of me for now.

"Jeremy Morris . . ." Ms. Ramirez warns.

"Doncha got gymnastics lessons to go to?"

"Naw, I'm just doing that on Fridays now." Since I was eight I have been going to this Bratislavan coach who tells me sometimes I'm going to be in the Olympics but I don't think so.

"Are you gonna do that school show with Mr. Yuk?" Jeremy asks.

And I giggle, hand over mouth. "Maybe. He met me in the front hall before homeroom. He wants me to show my high bar routine in class today."

Our gym teacher (whose name is Mr. Yahuniak but we call him Mr. Yuk because he always does the Poison Awareness speech) is planning some kind of exhibition at the end of the year.

"So you gonna do it?" I shrug. "No shit. I'm cutting after Spanish though."

"Maybe you can see it in June. If you're not expelled yet!"

"Jeremy, Ivan, silencio," commands Ms. Ramirez.

"You suck eggs," Favis whispers. He's on my right.

"Who wants a 72?" asks Ms. Ramirez like she is being generous. A 72 is the ultimate threat at Joe McCarthy Middle School. Shut the hell up and turn around you know. Or it gets back to Dad. "Repíte, clase: dos Coca-Colas, por favor."

"Dos Coca-Colas, por favor."

"Camarero?" asks Ms. Ramirez, all flirty thrusting back a hip. She twists to face the other side of our classroom. "Camarero?" Maybe they are stunned by her neon pink lips or her age spots or they think she is going crazy. She is not in a restaurant and they are not her waiters. Jeremy pivots back around like a second baseman. On the inside of his pants leg that big lump, tight on the fabric of his cords, stretching and growing like he is possessed. When he's on speed his eyes look like the girl's in the *Exorcist*. Like he is staring straight through you from a parallel universe. I wonder if he even wears underwear.

"Camarero, dos Coca-Colas, por favor," Ms. Ramirez orders.

"Camarero, dos Coca-Colas, por favor," we follow.

"Now before you all leave today," she says, looking anxiously at the clock, knowing that when the bell rings she can't stop us from mobbing out, "I want to remind you that it's Stranger Danger week. If a stranger comes up to you and tries to get you in his car, you know what to say, 'No!' Repeat class, 'No, I will not get in your car.'"

"No, I will not get in your car," we say. I think we all mean it: None of us would get in her car voluntarily, unless we were stealing it.

"No voy a salir contigo en tu caro!"

We try to repeat this and fail miserably. She pretends to be a Mexican sheriff. Jeremy lets me tick off the seconds on his sweet new LCD watch. With ten seconds left, Ms. Ramirez yells, "No adult should be touching your private parts except your doctor! If an adult other than your doctor touches your privates, that is rape!" Jeremy rolls his gold eyes and the bell drowns her out.

From here on in until stage crew we have different schedule cards. They get lunch and then gym with Mr. Davis, so they'll all be on The Funky List, which is a list of the boys who don't shower. For me it is gym with Mr. Yuk. Locker rooms. Naked boys. Then lunch. Our afternoon schedules are split, so I won't see the other Impostors till the last bell rings.

The rest of the crew is waiting for us in the entrance hall. We pass the metal detectors and turn right at the glassy main office. The last door on the right is the boys' entrance.

Favis and Dewey are making fun of Ms. Ramirez.

"Dos Coca-Colas, por favor," says Favis. "Dos Coca-Colas más. That lady's addicted to Coke."

"I'm addicted to some red pills Jer gave me second hour," Dewey tells us. He's straggling, waiting for Jeremy. Jeremy's at the bubbler emptying a soda can he spits in that he smuggles from class to class under his loose shirt. He can hide anything under a dirty T. He doesn't drink water ever. Jeremy drinks tobacco juice and Orange Crush. His skin and lips and tongue are orange.

"Dipstick, give me a wad," Favis says, coming from behind to cop a feel on the tin in Jeremy's back pocket. Fave pokes him in the ribs. Jeremy points a skeleton finger to his Walkman and that long thin smile of his mom's cuts his face. I know cuz I've been at their house for air band rehearsals and sleepovers. She has an awesome stereo and goes out on the weekends. Jer calms down when he listens to Quiet Riot, head nodding softly up and down, hair flapping the

Tiger Beat poster of Randy Rhodes on his bedroom wall. Otherwise he's all crazy, half-bald head shining, fucked-up crooked smile on his face. And the hair he still does have flops in dishwater clumps down the back of his head. Nobody knows what's wrong with him and nobody asks since he never talks about it. I kind of think he cares but tries not to show it. So hard.

"Hear you're flipping today," says Dewey.

"Thinking about it." He's my best friend since Cal stopped paying attention. "We never had gymnastics before," says Favis. "Didn't know this ghetto school had shit for shit."

"Mr. Yuk told me there was a whole back room filled with mats," I say to giggles. "He did. Shut the fuck up."

"I think I've seen that," says Favis. "It's in, like the very back of the gym. I guess they sometimes use it for—*wrestling*." He waves his cast around, full of graffiti signatures. Fave got his arm broken in wrestling about a month ago. By one of those big-ass muscular kids I am so afraid of.

"So when can we see your arm again?"

"One week, babe." He fake-socks me in the shoulder. "As you can see, I'm still pretty fuckin' powerful." We're at the cafetorium. "Mock chicken leg," Favis announces, nose toward the stoves.

"Break an arm," says Dewey. "Or a leg—good luck!"

They rush into line and flash me thumbs-up signs. I shuffle down the hall with a hungry feeling in my stomach. Those crematorium cooks can sure make mock chicken leg. By the time I'm across from the dish section, though, the smells of industrial floor cleanser and a hundred dirty trays wash across the hallway and mingle with locker-room Brut and gym clothes no one ever washes. My stomach gurgles all the time.

Now butterflies. Hope I know my routine. They probably won't be able to tell if I screw up anyway. Faster, closer to my gym locker. No one else in here—still have two minutes to get dressed after the warning bell, blasting through metal cubbies like a bomb drill. Practically tie my shoes together trying to get my shorts on! I can't wait so don't worry about hanging up my oxford and cords, just toss them in a small heap on the rusting locker base. Walk past Mr. Yuk's office, look away from its glass, if he were inside he would have been over to talk already.

I step out the back way to the gymnasium. Mr. Yahuniak is setting up a horizontal bar in the middle of the basketball court, kneeling down to connect a cord to a hook in the hardwood floor. As usual he's got on a baby-blue jumpsuit with pants flaring over his big floppy feet. Quite a sight when he overheats cuz he takes off the jacket and he's always got these huge sweat circles under the arms of his pastel polos. He bobs on the balls of his feet when he walks and cuz his pants flare so much the only part of his shoes you can see are the white plastic toecaps.

"This what you want me to use?"

"Hey, there you are!" He smiles big and bright, his eyes light up. His blonde hair covers his face like Jeremy's, if Jeremy had more if it. "This is the only place I can attach the supports. You could do parallel bars in the mat room, but more people will see you on the high bar."

"Sure, I don't care. Do we got any magnesium?"

He looks puzzled, like he's thinking, *What is this, earth science?*

Try again. "You know, chalk blocks? So my hands don't stick to the bar?"

"I'll ask Ms. M. She might have some old stuff hidden away, you know I don't do this much with the boys, but ever since you got here they have really shown an interest. I'll finish setting this up and then—" he pauses, tenses, tightens a cord. My bar in Waukesha is sure different. "Tell me what you have planned."

"Got a routine from Waukesha Tumblers. Kip to handstand. Then two giant swings. And then a real easy switch, and a reverse flip dismount."

"Gee, Eye, are you sure you want to do all that?" He's real excited.

"Why not? I do it every week five times full. Besides, I know what I'm doing. You're going to have to raise the bar, too. I can't bend my knees when I swing down—that's a form break."

"Well, I think I can do that. You coming to practice in the mornings next week?"

"If you can get me out of homeroom. That's when it is, right?"

"It's the only time we can do it." That's the bonus. In homeroom we're not allowed to talk or write notes, only supposed to read in the Book Nook and recite the pledge with the morning announcements. Our homeroom teacher Miss Z wears miniskirts and black lipstick and tall thin pointy heels. She's super-strict. We think she's secretly a dominatrix.

Ask him, "Is Pete doing it too?"

"He said he'd be there. He's a good tumbler." It's good to know there's at least one more boy with me. And Pete is cute, tan, blonde, short like me but solid instead of skinny. He goes steady with Moya and we all think she's the finest eighth grade girl. They take showers together! On the weekends, that's what Pete says. I could watch that like Mr. Yuk watches me.

Ever since springtime my first year here, Mr. Yuk has been paying extra attention to me. Back then I got elected for student council in my homeroom. He's the faculty advisor. He nominated me for secretary. I was voted in because nobody else wanted to take notes. After that he invited me to join his new committee to plan and perform these anti-drug/anti-vandalism skits for younger kids at other schools, during our school hours. I joined, thinking Jeremy would be jealous: a pass to miss class!

This year Mr. Yuk switched and took over my gym class from Mr. Davis.

I'm not positive when I told him I liked cars, but one day at the beginning of last year, he came to my homeroom to say hello to me. He told me he had some things in the hall to give me and got permission for me to look at them. 'Course I got made fun of real bad but went with him to the corridor. He'd brought two heavy shopping bags full of old *Motor Trend* and *Road & Track* magazines that he said I could have. It was pretty cool I guess but the latest models are better except for the Corvettes.

"I know you like cars," he had explained. Then we both grinned and shrugged. He helped me put the bags in my locker. What was I going to do with all these magazines? When I had gone back to class, I told the guys what he'd given me and they just looked at me like what's going on, Eye? None of us really understands why he likes me so much.

Mr. Yahuniak knows what happened this winter, which I barely talk about to anyone. Cal knows too but we hardly see each other anymore: he said he was sorry about it and put his arm around me but I couldn't feel him through our parkas. It was bitter cold and windy the day she died and he was eager to get out of our driveway. I tried to thank him but I couldn't make noise. The tears froze my lips shut. Inside, Dad does not talk about it. He doesn't want to cry again in front of me. Not even Jeremy knows.

When Mom was paralyzed in December she couldn't move but she could still hear everything. That's what the doctors said. Dad didn't cry until he heard that, or even much after, not even when the surgeon said she had some bad news. Mom was in Mexico digging up a lost city when the locals started dropping like flies. She got herself evacuated but only after six kids had already died. She puked herself into a coma on the plane back. When the docs opened her up to find out what was wrong they gave her an anesthetic she was allergic to, and her lungs stopped working. They said it looked like she'd eaten rat poison. We had one of our anti-drug presentations at some elementary school the day of her second operation. I didn't find out until after school, when Mr. Yuk read the note the office had left for him. He was the one who first told me she was paralyzed. He dropped me off at the hospital on his way home. I wanted him to come in with me but he wouldn't. I talked to Mom for twenty-five minutes before the machines went haywire. If she made it, I told her, I would run with my butterfly net and catch monarchs she could keep as pets. She looked collapsed and smashed, like a moth that's been banging into streetlights all night long.

Orange Crush

Don't try to make us feel better, I could tell Dad was thinking, as the doctors came to us after the third surgery. *Every time you take her away you screw her up worse.* Back then I could still read his mind. Sometimes it would come through so loud and clear I'd look around thinking other people heard his thoughts too. Since then, through the winter and so far this spring, he has hibernated in his den, and I can't read him at all.

My father can move but he can't hear anything. At home Dad works late into the night on nebulas and black holes. He is always in his study, open can of snuff on his junkyard desk, scribbling equations in ancient Greek. He only gets up after dinner to do sets on the chin-up bar stuck below the transom of the back door of their bedroom. Sometimes we do them together. Instead of talking, he counts. He counts how many breaths he takes, how many chin-ups we do, how fast my pulse is. Every night, before I go to bed, I stand in the doorway to his study and watch him slaving over his thick-lined paper, in a cloud of white cosmic dust from the lime-green Tupperware bowl of magnesium, muttering about red dwarves. I wave to him comically and say goodnight in my loudest cheeriest voice, but mostly he misses me. He misses us all now. Sometimes there is a delayed reaction, and I'll hear his voice as I walk back down the hall. And once in awhile he will call a goodnight, later, when he's locking up the house and sees my light under the door. But usually, he does not seem to know that I am there. It's not that I'm not good enough. It's just that I'm not enough. He is in a different dimension and there are so many particles besides my own. When I'm up there I shiver. It's like there's a ghost in the room.

Today I look sideways at Mr. Yuk, who pays quick attention. Sweat collects under his arms, darkening his shirt fabric like window trim as more kids enter the gym. "There," he says. "All set, I'll be right back with the chalk. Test it out?"

Ms. M cinches open the divider curtain. She talks to Mr. Yuk, nods her head. The girls start coming in slowly. Is Moya in their section?

Orange Crush

The gym bell rings and kids tuck their gold shirts into their red shorts and their red shirts into their gold shorts, scurrying out of the locker room doors like mice running from a broom. The girls aren't all there when Mr. Yuk gets back, but he starts anyway with a gymnastics lecture. It's time to concentrate on my routine. There's now a small piece of bright white magnesium chalk on the blue mat by Mr. Yuk's feet. He leads us through some stretching exercises after the lecture. About halfway through the class, he blows his whistle and I get my chance on the bar. The class fans out to the dividing curtain, which Ms. M has winched closed again, biceps flexing.

"Today Ivan is going to perform a bar routine. Circle up!"

Magnesium bricks are so huge and light they must come from another universe. Caking silt against palms and all my calluses, I move under the bar and Mr. Yuk moves with me.

"Do you need a spotter?" he asks. "A spotter is someone who supports the gymnast," he explains to the class.

"No, I'm fine," but he's spotting me anyway. "Really. I can jump." His long hands reach under my shoulders and hoist me quickly.

Hanging from the bar, I do a kip: swinging my toes to the bar and then kicking out while I muscle up so the bar's at my waist. Then I kick up into a handstand, edge forward, tense my stomach back into an underswing. My torque swings me back under again, and I carefully switch hands and kip once more so I'm back on top, facing the other way. So far so good. This bar's thick and smooth, like it's just been polished. I can barely get my hands around it. I look down at Mr. Yahuniak and the class, which is completely quiet for the first time ever.

"This bar is really slippery." Being short it's real cool to look down at everyone.

"Is it all right?" asks Mr. Yuk.

"I think so. I think it'll be all right. It's just really slippery. Greasy almost."

"If you don't think it will work, get off," he says. Just smile easy I think I can I know I can. "Ivan—"

Next move's the first giant swing: kick back up to a handstand and let myself fall back, using gravity to create enough speed to circle back over at the end. The class cheers. My eyes bear down on the bar. I keep a straight body line, drop back into another sweeping circle, thinking about the flip at the dismount. When I do giant swings I feel like an electron racing around a molecule. My feet clear the plastic below me. My toes are forty-five degrees from the ground. At the peak of acceleration my hands slip and fingers extend, peeling off the thick metal, out of orbit. Air rushes like rivers, ninety eyes blurring by, the mat flies past, and I dive into an empty pool.

My landing is all parts at once, fifteen feet from the bar, on the court next to the free-throw line. There's no way to get up. I'm shocked but sure everything's all right, nothing's broken, still in one piece.

Just another fall.

I hear screaming and friends running over.

"Eye, don't move, are you okay, say something!" I open eyes to Mr. Yahuniak. I'm not going to cry I'm not, so don't say anything, because it hurts, because he has run over so fast so I play hard, squinting at him, like a beaver making a dam. Ms. M herds kids away, her whistle and drill instructions shrill, over the screams: "C'mon, girls, *out.*" Mr. Yuk rasps, too soft for me to hear. I feel his dejection and don't want it at all.

I'm shouting. "I'm all right! I'm OK! I'll get up by myself."

"You guys can go early," he says.

I shut my eyes, sense the boys sticking around. Usually they're half-dressed ten seconds after he says that.

"Get outta here, hit the showers," he growls, "Ivan will be all right." Tennis shoes squeak across the floor to the locker rooms. "Do you think you can get up?"

"Ready." He holds my hands, and so slowly I twist onto my back from the sideways landing position. I must look like a crashed plane. "Arms are good." Mr. Yahuniak raises me onto wobbling feet and I don't know where my body is anymore. I fall against him, he takes hold of my shoulders and tips me over, carries me like a baby into his office. He lays me across his desk, flicks the blinds shut. Running showers sound like laughter, far away. I hear him yell at some kids, jangle his keys, toe-bounce off. Then quiet, lids shut tight, thinking of home—lying in bed, Jeremy prancing around my room synchronizing his face to his favorite Ratt song:

> *Round and round, your love will find a way,*
> *   just give it time.*
> *Round and round, what comes around goes around,*
> *   I'll tell you why. . . .*

I'm still shaking uncontrollably. My stomach has gone right through my hands.

The door sighs open and the lock clicks, he's back. Prone on the cold metal desk, head immobile, my eyes are closed.

Mr. Yuk flips back my medical bracelet so he can read the inscription. On the front there are two red snakes twirling around a cross.

"You're allergic to Anectine? What's that?"

"Muscle relaxant."

"What happens?"

"If they give it to me I won't be able to breathe on my own. It's because I have a pseudocholinesterase deficiency. My mom has it too. Had it. That's why she stopped breathing," I quaver to the ceiling like each dot in the soundproof tile's a new friend. "And by then it was just too late . . ."

His hands tap softly on knees, checking for reflexes, knocking without a hammer. He says the bumps on my side are starting to swell. "Where does it hurt?"

"Everywhere."

"You're wheezing. Take off your shirt so I can see your ribs, they could be cracked."

He's anxious, trembling a little. My fall's really shaken him.

"Does it hurt here?" he is asking. "Here?" Fingertips soar over my belly like summer monarchs flying in the backyard. I think of them landing in Mom's wavy red hair but he never touches down. "Pulse

22

feels good . . . no irregularities. I've got to see that everything is intact, let's take your shorts . . . off." He's breathing strange like me.

Now I know he won't stop. I start getting hard. Flesh presses against my Hanes like a helium balloon bumps up to the ceiling, feeling for a way to go higher. Where did all the air go? You can jump twenty feet high on the moon, and I feel weightless when his hands glide by my stomach. He takes off my shorts, trying not to move my spine at all. It is starting not to hurt anymore. I tell him.

"It doesn't hurt anymore," I whisper. He slides my underwear to the top of my thighs.

"You're so lucky you're all right," he says, but means something else, something more.

I'm embarrassed and everything's red. Nothing hurts anymore when he stares. He is healing by looking.

My penis can flex back and forth. It makes a slapping sound when it smacks my stomach. I wonder if he is going to touch me there and rape me. I try to thrust my pelvis toward him but it won't really move. The only parts I can move are my lips and my dick.

"Does this hurt?" he says, quiet and high and hoarse, like he just sucked helium straight from the tank. He swallows. He is circling my balls with his fingers. It makes me shake so hard I almost fall off the desk. He can make me move again. I think I am Pinocchio. He puts a hand on my stomach to hold me down. "That hurts a lot?"

"It doesn't hurt," I whisper. "It just tickles like nuts." I flex back and forth one more time.

"What about your penis," he asks. "Does it hurt?"

"It feels weird." I shut my eyes tight. I want him to touch the one part of me that feels good. I feel for his hand with my penis but he is stronger than me and grabs my wrist instead. "But it feels good weird not bad weird."

"It looks fine," he says to me. His hand is tight around my bones, like a child holding fast to a balloon so it will not fly away.

"You can rape me again to make sure," I whisper. I want him to know it's OK. I want to know why my dick feels so weird and so hard. And he rips my wrist from his hand and the medical bracelet hits the table and the door squeals open. Glass bangs as it slams shut, and then silence. The showers are off and there is no more laughter, just the distant battle of closing stuffed lockers.

When he doesn't come back, when I know he won't while I'm there, I very slowly put my gym clothes back on. Only as I try to stand do I know how bad it is and I have to grind my teeth together in order not to cry. I scrape my body off his desk, crawl across the floor, limp down the hallway. I don't know why he left. He already raped me anyway by touching my balls and I said it was OK. Maybe he loves me? I pass the crematorium but someone says they closed five minutes ago. My belly's killing me, my chest. Face in my hands, I crumple to the green linoleum, double over.

Jeremy sees me. He's walking to the boys' locker room.

"Hey, Eye, how are you, we heard it all, are you—"

I can't look up, slumped against the wall. Tears fill my eyes, slink down cheeks one by one.

"Ivan?" he tries again. "Are you all right? I'm really sorry." He wipes my face with his long dry palm.

"Me. There's no more food. I crashed onto the floor in front of everybody. McCarthy *sucks*." The only way to keep from screaming is to speak real soft. "I thought you were gonna skip."

"Changed my mind. Besides Cap said he could sell me some speed seventh hour. Here," he says, reaching into a paper bag. He kneels down on the floor and I watch the lump slither along one leg of his corduroys. "Have an apple. You want some Orange Crush?"

"Thanks. Have you seen the other Impostors?"

"I heard they were outside."

"Dewey and Favis are probably smoking across the street. Getting buzzed." I manage a wavering laugh. "So do people think I'm real weak now?" I ask. It comes out like a moan, like someone dying.

"From what I heard you were never gonna walk again. So I think you're a hero for making it down the hall." The warning bell rings. He looks at me concerned. "If I don't get in there, Mr. Davis will

24

have my ass on a platter." He stands up and turns around, wiggles his butt for me. "Hey, you still got my watch?" He holds out his hands.

I unlatch the metal from the rubber and let the crumbling plastic fall into Jeremy's palms. The cover's smashed and the numbers and dates are crazy, months and hours and seconds melting into each other and happening all at once.

His apple hurts my jaws. Kids come over, snicker and tease and ask how I'm doing. Someone fronts me a Snickers. Don't know how I can take it from them cuz I'm in my own world.

The clocks tick so loudly when school's fifteen minutes from ending. Maybe I'll bail on stage crew and get home before Dad and lie down in my bunk bed and pretend to smell Mom cooking kohl-rabi soup.

"Oh, no!" I say loudly, surprising myself.

"What's wrong?" My social studies sub looks suspiciously through his thick tinted glasses at me, then his seat chart. "Ivan?"

I move up towards him. "I need to get my street clothes!"

We're only reading, so it's all right with him. I jerk down the empty hallways to the gym, look for Mr. Yuk inside the locker room again. His office is locked. There's no sound from inside, the blinds still down, me reflecting faintly in the glass like a specter from Dungeons and Dragons. I want to tell him he doesn't have to worry about raping me. I write a note saying that I liked it and wouldn't report it and there was a good reason for him to do it, and besides, I don't think of him as a stranger but as a friend. I think of leaving it under the door, but then I get worried Mr. Davis will find it by mistake, so I just crumple it up and throw it away. He's not in the gym either, as far as I can see from the back door window. There's nobody here. I can do what I want, no one's looking at me.

I see myself through the glass, on the table, examined. Surveyed like an archaeological dig, some old skeleton. Sitting down on a bench by my locker, I test the combination, twist it around to waste time. When the piece slips into the right notch, I creak open the door, change back into my wrinkled clothes from the bottom of my locker and almost don't hurt myself again. Quiet like sitting Shiva for Mom after Dad pulled the plug. I shudder and it happened to me. A few hours ago naked before him. Injun Joe was a grave robber you know but still he was a pretty good guy.

Look again at me. Take as much as you want. Take as much time.

But from now on, he will not meet my eyes. He can make me disappear.

That summer the world falls away. In its place come sunny afternoons smoking pot in Jeremy's apartment, walking down the train tracks to the Oriental to sneak into *Cabaret*. In July we go to the Quiet Riot show at Mecca, downtown.

At adjacent urinals Jeremy whispers, "That's a fag." He points to the man beside him, who zips up and leaves.

"How do you know?" I ask, but I guess I already know the answer.

"He's just like the guys on my paper route," he shrugs. He shakes the rest of his piss into the porcelain. "The way he was looking at me. You ever think of being a paperboy? It's good money."

I go back to the restroom three times but I don't see any more fags there.

August slips down the riverbank to the paper plant, huffing spray paint, untying haystacks of porn on the shore. Jeremy presses his silver fist into my stomach as I hold my arms above my head. Blood slowly diffuses and I feel the tingle of carbon dioxide like a mainline of cold water down my arms, and black out on the mud, Jeremy shielding my head.

That September his mom sends him to military school somewhere near Sheboygan. He must have gotten caught doing something—scamming his customers, stealing his mom's drugs—but I never find out what. My memories of him will fade into static, like a radiocast of the Brewers on a muggy summer night—cold Crush on the counter, tears of condensation on the can, sweat beads on his forehead, 1985.

Love Maps

The last present my mother gave me was a paperback called *What's Happening to Me?* It was, of course, about puberty. I knelt in the hallway over a centerfold of a naked youth at successive stages of sexual maturity. I wasn't sure then if it was a photo or a sketch. My guess now is that it was a pointillist illustration based on photographs. When I saw the boy in the middle I fell in love. I took him upstairs to the laundry room mirror, to compare. We were the same, only my dick was rock hard. I thought, *What's happening to me?*

By the time I was sixteen, my train was even more off-track. When I cut class or procrastinated to avoid my biology assignments, I killed time flipping through the card catalogues at the local college library. In short order, I discovered "puberty—boys—rites of passage," and "sexual abuse—males—case studies," and "homosexuality—Greece." After I had exhausted these resources, I tried the kiosk of computer screens near the reference desk, keying "art and boys and nudes," and "Klinefelter's syndrome," and "pederasty," and—when I got more advanced—"intergenerational male intimacy," which yielded detailed Dutch research that left me contending with certain inch-to-centimeter ratios.

One icy night, when I had six weeks' worth of homework due, I sprinted the short blocks from home to the library in my winter coat and soccer shorts, to wake myself up. There I tapped into a CD-ROM, the Medline, and came up with a reference to "priapism and adolescence" that promised black-and-white prints of synthetic growth hormone side effects. The journal in question was located in Compact Shelving, the electronically separable stacks deep in the basement. I found my parameters and pressed the Operate button on the elevator box wired into the side of the metal bookshelf. A green light flashed. As long as I fingered the button, the stacks hummed to life, parting for me, acquiescent as passed-out friends. I headed down the newly created aisle, squinting for the *American Journal of Diseases in Children*.

Vaulted within five-hundred microthin pages was a doctor, frozen, grasping teen male genitalia, like a spokesmodel displaying items up for bids on "The Price Is Right"—it's a priapic fifteen-year-old with delayed maturation! Start the bidding at $200! My heart sank to my guts, thumped into my prostate, and surged through my dick as I carried the book to the back of the basement, between the last closed stack and the blank stucco wall. I tugged my blue checkered soccer shorts under my balls, and jacked off alongside the fondled specimen.

A whim impelled me back over the tracks to examine the journal's annual indices. In the 1940s, Earle Reynolds and Janet Wines had taken thousands of pictures of fifty-nine boys from Yellow Springs, Ohio, some of which appeared in 1951, under "Physical Changes Associated with Adolescence in Boys." The seven sizes of the flaccid penis fascinated me. "We have also taken a few measurements of both stretched and erect penis," they wrote. "In four boys, there is a history of semi-erections at a number of visits. This is noted routinely on the physical examination record, and can also be seen readily in the photographs."

That night, I smeared semen on my tie-dyed boxers; over a library card slipped from its slot on the topside of the rack; across old folio maps crinkling on the black plastic shelf to my left. I'd never seen so much sperm. Hell, I'd never seen any; my girlfriend was always gobbling mine up or jerking me off in the dark. I was confused, this first night I'd successfully masturbated: what did I need Laverne for now? My shorts slapped my abs as I slam-danced through the footnotes, hot on the trail. My eyes flashed on one title—*Somatic Development of Boys,* by Stolz & Stolz: MacMillan, 1951.

A whole book! I was sure that if I found the Stolzes, I'd never need anyone else. I thought, I must have this book!

The Milwaukee libraries never had Stolz, but I memorized its Dewey decimal number, 612.661, and thus began my obsessive quest. From that night on, whirring stacks gave me erections. I learned to find joy in the permanent shelves, discovering *The Linked Ring: The Secession Movement in British Photography, 1892–1910,* which included some F. Holland Day expatriate scenes, listless surreal prints of unclad, wild youngsters emulating woodsy saints. I developed a fondness for case studies of abused kids, the only accounts I could find of boys having sex with other males. I shielded Theo Sandfort's *The Sexual Aspect of Paedophile Relations: The Experience of 25 Boys,* held it close to John Money's *Love Maps* and *Paraphilia,* let *The Sexual Offender and His Offenses* kiss *The Boys of Boise.*

Sometimes I scaled locked doors and climbed into the study rooms on the library's second and third floors; there was a gap between the wooden doors and the acoustic ceiling that I could squeeze through, muscling up and then rappelling down onto the desk, where I'd pop open a portfolio from the 1932 *Journal of Nervous and Mental Disease.* Entitled "The Secondary Sex Characteristics of Boys in Adolescence," the article was laden with soft, fuzzy photos of cherubic, denuded guys standing side by side under such captions as, "testicular size in this group varied from small almond to large walnut." Into the trash can I came.

My personal fave was Frank Shuttleworth's 1949 piece in the *Monographs for Social Research in Child Development*, "The Adolescent Period: A Graphic Atlas." As soon as I read the abstract— "consists entirely of half-tone reproductions of photographs of nude children, mostly serial photographs taken at different ages"—I clutched the burlap backing and bounded blindly for cover in a three-walled, corner carrel. I thought of Toby, a freshman in my homeroom, as I obsessed over Shuttleworth's "late-maturer," a pasty kid whose face was obscured by a black box painted over it. Full-frontal and biannual from 11.5 to 17.1 years, he stood anal-receptive, juxtaposed to front the taller "early-maturer," a similarly defaced skinny kid. I copied their measurable attributes into my notebook, robotic. Then I took my blue Bic and wrote on the carrel's wooden wall:

"I'm 16, brown hair + eyes, 5'7'', 135 lbs, sparse copper pubic hair, none under my arms. If interested," and then my pen gave out.

I yearned for the opportunity to compare myself to a real, flesh-and-blood guy. In high school I got glances from one older kid in the weight room and wanted him to ask me out. Or something. I trailed him one day past rotting piers and chalk-white boulders on Lake Michigan's shore, both of us alone, awash in the stench of poisoned alewives. But nothing came of it. Books were more dependable.

Invisibility makes you want to be seen. I stalked a footnote all the way to the West Side, past Milwaukee County Stadium to the Medical College of Wisconsin. There I found a one-of-a-kind folio supplement to an adolescence textbook: two European boys in oversize sepia stared back at me, stuck in 1964. In a trance I took the poster to the communal study table. Two white-haired doctors sat at each head, engrossed in thick journals. Next to me, a bald-spotted researcher jotted wet notes; across, a blonde female doc skimmed restlessly. I pried open the Dutch boys like a bucket of paint and moved my chair as far under the table as I could before my stomach hit the edge. I unzipped one flange at a time, breathed in intermittent silent gasps. My cock hit the underside of the table and I dragged it against its own streaking effluvium and along the smooth grain. I left stalactites sweeter than bubble gum. How could no one have noticed?

Sometimes I found books I wanted, like *Control of the Onset of Puberty,* or J. M. Tanner's *Growth in Adolescence,* only to see that certain pictures had been removed with razor blades. The technique seemed so cold. I preferred to fold them over, crease them slowly, gently tear the boys away.

To exact revenge against the vandals, or maybe jealously wanting the boys all to myself, I started hiding my captives inside my official high school folder, the one they gave us in homeroom, with an etching of our prison silk-screened in blue on the cover. The ripped-out photos, musty with age, gave the folder the bitter-almond smell of cyanide. I liked to carry it down into my house's dank cellar and leaf through it, like the wind, during tornado warnings.

On cold winter afternoons, in my junior year of high school, I'd get home two hours before Dad. That left me and the cat, and Amaranth went outside as soon as I got home, even though it was freezing. It was warm in the house.

The house was big and brick. In warm months it was covered with ivy. The third floor went completely unused. We used to rent it out to college students but my mom didn't like the creaks above her bedroom when she was trying to sleep. Dad told me he was thinking of renting it out again. For now, his weight equipment was up there, and my grandfather's love seat. He died right after I got back from DC, nine months before my mother. The madras couch fronted three windows that looked over the boulevard. The afternoon sun lay in shafts on the cushions, which were laced with white cat fur. I imagined that the dust helices inside these sun shafts were interplanetary beams that would atomize me, transport me to ecstasy, and return me unharmed and happy.

For years after she died, until I moved out, Mom's no-nonsense bras were still draped on the rod in her closet; her bright white Mexican blouses were hanging in the laundry room; her favorite taupe pumps tripped me up in the vestibule. I brought her tall, swinging mirror upstairs to witness my transformation, then sprawled on the couch to experiment. I wanted to see my down light up in the flares that made it through the window and the plastic storm in front of it. The small red patch of hair I'd grown was ablaze. Thoughts disappeared in the shaft of January sunlight. Me: skin and shadow, sperm, rising and falling, restrained only by breath, muscle, and gravity.

Every molecule in me strained to be seen. I wanted those two dimensions to replicate through some ancient, forgotten mitosis, so that the attic was an orgy of fun-house mirrors and naked teenagers like me. I wished someone would take pictures of me. I wondered what it would be like to strip on stage, pretended to be a stripper, and came again minutes later in my skimpiest white briefs, or my mom's blue one-piece, straps slipped off the shoulders, vulva-liner scrunched into my ass. In the audience were men of all shapes, colors, ages. Their faces mattered much less than their presence.

That year my dad described a wormhole to me.

"There are enormous forces at work in space, Ivan," he'd say. "Now, a wormhole is an almost infinitesimally small passageway that opens at one end in the space-time continuum, and comes out at another part of space-time."

"Like Pac-Man?"

I pretended I could go into a wormhole and wind up somewhere else. That's where my body went, under the sun-shaft, and inside the mirror. The trick was where and when to come out, and I had no idea how to control that. When my dad was in the garage, tinkering with the cars (an old Volvo with a hole in the floor, and then a '70s model Ford, a detective car), I would fantasize that he was building a time machine just for me.

I wanted to be eight again, but I didn't know why.

Back when I was eight, my dad was addicted to Pac-Man, and especially, Ms. Pac-Man. It got to the point where he wouldn't stop playing to order our Blizzards at Dairy Queen. Something about the arcade must have soothed this distant, fiery man with the red beard:

the way you could go in one side and out the other, or the way you could munch the ghosts. They scared me, their blinking transparency, their demonic chatter. How could they endlessly regenerate? Why couldn't you get rid of them for good?

And what if you never came out the other side? What if you got stuck in that nowhere? Where would you be then?

In my mother's old bathroom, cleaning up. I'd take forever because there were so many things there. I had to smell them all before leaving. I began with the constants, the basics: Crest Regular. It was polite but not as good-natured and fresh as the Extra gum in the blue pack. The tampons in the trash were wrapped in brown paper bags, old and dry and withered. When I stuck my nose into their fibers I could smell her again, the faint reminder of the heavy warm wave under her sheets in the morning, before Dad wouldn't let me anymore. ("Your father thinks you're too old for that," my mother whispered apologetically, when I was nine.) *Things are different now,* said the mélange of her old deodorant and the shaving gel she used to use and her stuff that made my hair real sleek after showers. I spent whole afternoons looking for her perfume, but it was the only thing of hers that disappeared. Enveloped in the melancholy mist of hairspray, I'd leave a note for Dad and walk to pick up Laverne to see a matinee. I'd wear my most elastic sweatpants, no undies. She'd wear tartan skirts and thin panties. The grand old Oriental was big and dark enough for our clandestine hand jobs. As the credits rolled I'd draw my fingers to my face, pretending to stifle a yawn. They smelled like my mother's side of the bed.

At night, naked, in my bed, Dad snoring through the wall, I'd make the world fall away again. I didn't need Jeremy to gut-bust me anymore. If I lay there long enough with my eyes closed the walls retreated and I could travel anywhere. I flew outside and down the boulevard to the lake and chased the moonbeam to Chicago, the land where I squirmed out of her. And sometimes my mother would come to me in the night, weightless as a shadow, her face gray and decaying, skin trailing in flayed strips like a tie in the wind. *What is it like to be dead?* I asked her, under my eyes and my breath. She opened her mouth and neon butterflies flew out in a rainbow. *Lepidoptera* always had an affinity for her, and she for them. They'd alight on her shoulder when she sat in the backyard. Those afternoons I knew she was a butterfly herself: her fragile spine, freckles coloring her cheeks the spotty tan of monarch wings. In this flapping cloud she turned around and disappeared again.

The Salmon Capital of the World

The summer I turned twenty I fell in love with traveling and a boy named Sean. We lived in a tent made from plywood and pallets and stolen blue tarpaulins. We worked the same line in an Alaskan fish factory. We watched the river for biplanes and rock cod and swooping black cormorants. We climbed a mountain and stashed red wine in the snow. When we weren't working Sean would take off the only shirt he ever wore. He was a quiet mousy boy about 5′5′′. His mother had recently killed herself. He never told us how. He had shiny white canines, thin black eyebrows, a small short nose, and long hazel eyes. His hair was fine and oily and dishwater blonde and flopped over his face so he had to wear a hairnet when he excised the skulls before the tops went on the cans.

That May I'd returned briefly to Wisconsin from a college in Pennsylvania, planning to spend the summer at home. My prospects distressed me. I thought I might work pizza delivery again, if only I hadn't crashed the Ford into a parked Jeep the previous July, craning out the passenger side to catch an address. You should never keep driving when you're halfway out of the car. The guy who ordered the large pepperoni and mushrooms that had since slid into its own paste also owned the dented Jeep. *The good news is your pizza's here. The bad news is it's a wreck and so's your car.* We settled the score in his backyard for the contents of my apron. I was still unsettled.

And, I figured, I could paint houses but for my penchant of falling off ladders. Soon after retiring from pizza delivery, I sprayed white window trim into a hornets' nest. Flying stinging creatures terrified me. The next house was an old Victorian mansion in a suburb we called White Folks Bay. I was scraping a second-story soffit and stretched too far. You should never paint when you're halfway off a ladder, but anyone can make that mistake. The real trick is to make it all fall on you when you go: stepladder, roller, edging stick, brush, big open bucket of paint. My boss (my friend Trance's big brother) fired me immediately the second time. "We do windows, not fucking shingles and sidewalks," Cuong said sadly, after checking my pulse. It seemed to me that I was more or less out of options.

My sex life was hopeless. The only gay guys I met were the ones in park bathrooms redolent with urinal discs and old piss. Flushing meant a cop or a straight guy was coming. All those rushing toilets made me feel hapless and nervous, wanting more. Two ex-girlfriends from high school had moved on to other cities and boys. I didn't have a lot of friends.

Trance (officially Tran, my old high school soccer teammate), had been growing hydroponic pot in his basement for several months. We met for basketball in late May, when I was trying to figure out how to spend the next few months. Dewey joined us on my old elementary school playground. We played hustle, first to twenty-one wins.

"Want to come over and landscape later then?" Trance asked. "Don't worry, no house painting in the plans." He cracked a fucked-up Mona Lisa with too much sly and not enough coy and drove the hoop.

I let him go, watched his fat ass catch spring sun through blue shorts; then blocked his shit from behind. I thought about depantsing him but worried Dewey would take it the wrong way. Or the right way.

I found the ball and swiveled to locate Dewey's gawky pitchers' frame. When we were twelve in art class I'd longed to run a thumb along the curved track of his angel's mark, the space between his stub nose and wide lips. I wanted to turn him into a statue because he was so quiet most of the time. But when he did talk he'd crack us all up, and even then he had a great hook shot, so I wouldn't have wanted Dew frozen in time for more than a few minutes. Instead, I stuck close to his side.

"If you need some help trimming bushes, we're always glad to assist," Dew grinned, shrugging his assent. "Just don't make me move furniture."

"What time ya want us?" I asked, and pulled up for a jumper. Trance lunged, his arms around my face. His fingertips stretched to me, our hands almost touching. I just wanted him to hug me so I could find out for sure if his neck smelled like kimchi.

Trance had been sharing an apartment with a punk kid named Hash who'd been hot as shit when he was fifteen but now resembled Jesus. Not really my thing, although He has his following. He was gone that night. Trance took us down to the basement, which we could smell from the front door, the humid breath of the sun beating down after a warm thunderstorm. Golf-course-green plants bloomed in rows under bright humming tubes. We picked the most mature tendrils we could find, microwaved them, and smoked. Dewey dispensed three white paper squares and we dissolved them together, one under each tongue.

The three of us went out night-driving in the hail-scarred hatchback my dad bought for cheap after my incident with the Jeep. We crept through the midnight mists and ghostly dew of Riverside Park. Dewey slid in the Pixies: *This ain't no holiday, but it always works out this way: Here I am with my hand.* I wondered whether men were in the bathrooms jerking off. A cop pulled us over. Trance hid the bong between his legs. I guessed I'd been swerving.

"Funny smell in there," the cop said. I didn't look at him but imagined he was wearing sunglasses in the dead of night. His sirens were pretty and flashy, like an under-twenty-one club. Dewey turned down the volume.

"Yeah, that's true," I agreed.

"Be careful," he said. I nodded my head vigorously, and he left. Trance was green in the backseat. The sky was pink, and Dewey was white like marble. After the cop left everything was black and silent, like he'd turned off the TV.

When we got back to the flat Trance popped in a movie. He was talking a lot but it wasn't coherent or I couldn't hear. The only scene I remember was two white men fucking a small black girl with a Coke bottle. My boys were entranced. We tuned into a crime show about a California psychopath who picked up boys by offering them drugs. "Fucker should have his balls cut off, that's what they should do, castrate those homos," said Trance, watching an actor dig a shallow grave. "Fuck that short-eyed piece of shit," added Dewey. *How can you treat boys that way?* I marveled, stimulated by a teenage sex slave in the mystery man's mobile dungeon. *You got some shit to ponder, going from chicken to wolf and denying it all this time,* I told myself, and the customized van careened into the sunset.

My stomach walls fended off a series of small explosions and I lurched into the bathroom. Shit bubbled from me like the Milwaukee River, sludgy and pungent. To add certain insult, a wall mirror was set across from the toilet. My face turned mauve in slow waves. I heard the locks and dams of my blood in my ears. I wanted to be more alive than this. I remembered what a college friend had told me about a fishing village in Alaska.

The next afternoon I stumbled out of bed and called the physics department, got Dad, and told him I was going to the Southeast Passage, off the coast of British Columbia, to fish for halibut. I tried hard to sound like I knew what I was talking about. He was thinking of gravitational forces held by stars too far away to see by telescope, and only known to exist by their absence, the wobble of light around them. He absent-mindedly agreed to advance me a frequent flyer ticket if I paid him back on my return.

"You are legless," I wrote on a Post-it in his room, "like the old dining room table propped against your bedroom wall, waiting to be moved out." Then I packed a sleeping bag, an army tent, and lots of T-shirts. A week later I found myself ducking out of a propeller plane onto a sunny runway twenty-six hundred miles away.

Ketchikan was the first stop. The rest of the passengers were going back to other islands, like Sitka, or getting off at the end of the line in Juneau, where the Tongass Narrows, which starts in Prince Rupert Sound, meets the mainland. The narrows was like an enormously wide river, and I was on the wrong side—Gravina Island, home of the jet strip. I hoisted my blue nylon body bag over my shoulder and lugged it across the gray planked causeway to Revilla-gigedo Island. Brown, white-capped mountains greeted me, the blue of the narrows, the red brick of the town.

It was a mile walk into Ketchikan. Ships cruised lazily under the bridge, mostly going northwest. A small red tugboat, heading home; an enormous white cruise ship docking into port, the lights of shops beside it; a long gray schooner, as flat and sleek as a kayak; two dark green trawlers with bodies like pick-up trucks, trailing fishnets like racy bridal trains. I watched them slide under the bridge and re-emerge and wished I were on one, wrapping thick ropes around bolted brass knuckles. My plan was to pound the pavement and bull-shit about fish with handsome, rugged skippers, real men of the sea. I'd never fished before in my life. The lakes at home were poisoned.

I stopped at the first restaurant on the other bank of the Tongass, ordered chili, stuffed a handful of Saltines into my pockets, and asked where the hostel was.

Since I'd come with what I had, about three hundred bucks, I didn't want to pay for lodging too long. In the men's dorm I soon learned from Randy, a scraggly, dog-tagged, stale-jeaned caricature of a Vietnam vet, that one of the local fisheries ran a free tent city. I asked whether he was going to work there. "I'd kill myself before I worked another factory job," he said, and tried to sell me a gun he'd smuggled up from Spokane. Besides, he added, with a sort of dismal scorn, the fishermen were on strike, and when the fishermen were striking there wasn't any work from Ketchikan to Kodiak. To shake off these doldrums, I wandered alone into the purpling twilight and made my way to the bars along the Narrows.

In my wallet was a fake ID that had served as an amulet since I was sixteen. A friend had painted a posterboard with a red picture box and appropriate stencils; Trance then swiped several holographic state laminates from the Department of Motor Vehicles. He sold them for ten bucks each. The resulting product wasn't exactly professional, but it satisfied bartender requisite. Though I hadn't even started to shave, nobody back home questioned that I wasn't really a man in his mid-twenties named Peter Turner . . . drinking with a pack of other striplings with the same name. They were just happy for the business.

That first night in Alaska I wasn't even grilled about my birth date. I drank Mezcal and watched the Bulls run through the Lakers in Michael Jordan's first trip to the Finals. There weren't any women in the bar or on the streets. The air was warm and musty and flushed and communal with sweat and testosterone and drunkenness. I called my father from a pay phone outside in the clear twinkling night, and told him I was okay and safe under a ceiling of the brightest stars I'd ever seen. It looked like someone had taken a broom to the sky, swept clean the cobwebs, and polished the suns.

When all color was gone from the sky, I returned to the hostel and found the men's bathroom. The shower was running so I brushed my teeth slowly, thoroughly. My heart was jumping out of its cage and I wanted to tear free the curtain and suck off whomever was in there. I rinsed my mouth several times. Finally the shower stopped; there was humming and drying and the artificial sweet scent of shampoo. A compact young man with blue eyes stepped out, clad in white boxers.

"Hey!" he smiled. "Matt Luciano." His chest was smooth and wet and tight. "From San Diego."

"Ivan. From Milwaukee."

We shook. "Hey, hey!" he said. "Here to fish?"

"Looking for anything, really. You staying in the dorm?"

"Just got in today!"

"Me too," I replied.

Matt threw on some sweats and a T-shirt and we walked downstairs. Randy was back, and card-players were grumbling. Amid whispers and the smoky tang of men I fell asleep.

The next morning was warm and sunny, and I walked around two sets of docks, moving from pier to pier and admiring the vessels, then amusing a succession of skippers by asking whether I could be their cabin boy. Gulls whooped war cries and dove into the brink. Biplanes bounced two, three, four times onto the skim, then settled, bobbing softly on the waves. I picked up a map of the island at a tourist trap near the Love Boat dock and bought a cup of coffee from a chatty vendor named Greg. I walked to the Department of Motor Vehicles and uneventfully exchanged my fake ID for a real one. My friendly civil servant decided that I was most likely to live in Tent City. "That's where they all wind up," she said, handing me my new identity and address: 735 Stedman Avenue, Ketchikan, 99950. On the walk back I pretended I was in the Witness Protection Program.

Downtown, where Tongass Avenue, the two-lane thruway, turns into a square, I saw Matt and Randy sitting with two other guys at a picnic table overlooking Ketchikan Creek. Matt introduced me to Dwayne, a tall spindly black man from Fresno, and Sean, a short white kid from Washington. I ordered a fried fish sandwich from an outdoor vendor and sidled up. Matt and Randy were just leaving, looking secretive. Dwayne and Sean were about to scour the fish factories to learn about jobs in the offing. Thinking I might find out where I now officially lived, I agreed to join forces.

Sean had also fruitlessly pounded the docks, and Dwayne hadn't had any luck with the fisheries nearby. The processing plants relied on locally caught fish, and the unified fishermen's strike for higher salmon prices had already delayed the start of the high season.

Paralleling the narrows, we walked three miles southeast down Tongass Avenue, passing a small fish factory, a few churches, and two dozen bars. Dwayne's strides were long and deliberate. Sean skipped to keep up, and I kept tripping over my shoelaces. We took a left, up the steep hillside at the base of Deer Mountain, and climbed a set of a wooden stairs set into the cliff that led to a Tlingit totem pole preserve. According to a wooden plaque, Civilian Conservation Corps campers created the monument in the 1930s. The older poles were thirty feet tall and their reds had faded to rust, deities eroded, their colors soaked too deep into the wood or bleached out by the sun. A dirt path from the poles wound through feathery Sitka pines into a rambling hillside park. Deer Mountain loomed snowcapped above a grassy plateau. We didn't talk that much, listening to the birds and the sounds our feet made walking through. Another path led back to the road. Dwayne and I consulted the map, which made a big deal out of tourist shops, grocery stores, and monuments, but wasn't much good for factories. Sean stuck out a thumb on the southeast side of Tongass.

An orange, old-style Mack cab squeaked to a stop on the shoulder.

"Well, what the hell are you waiting for?" the driver asked, craning his neck out the passenger side. I flinched involuntarily. "Hop in!" He turned his whole head to say hello, but only one eye moved. Sean jumped up and in, nestling close to the driver and looking at us with a smirk. Dwayne shrugged and joined them in the front seat, saving a sliver of vinyl for me by the door. Our ride revved up slow and asked where we were headed.

"Stedman Avenue."

"Can't say I know any street names. Sure can't see them anyway! Only got one eye, and we don't know how well that one works! This sucker's from 1973, but don't you think she still looks good?"

"Does he mean the eye or the truck?" Sean asked.

"Rig looks great," Dwayne offered.

"She's a steady one, sure as the salmon spawn. What's it near?" he asked.

I watched the plumes of black exhaust spouting from the pipe on the wheel well next to me. Dwayne nudged me and I pulled out the map. "Oh. It's a half-mile south of Tatsuda's Supermarket, on the left."

"Well hell, only thing around there's Farwest Fisheries, and that's right here." We lurched to rickety entropy on the gravel shoulder, next to a large, open chain link fence. The truck door wouldn't open. I had a quick anxiety attack about being drawn and quartered by a man with one glass eye.

"Open it from the outside," Dwayne suggested, and in my haste I planted my forearm into the sizzling vertical exhaust and screamed bloody murder. Sean politely said our thanks. There was an enormous, quiet factory to the right, stretching four hundred yards to the narrows. To the left was a large empty sandlot, its path to the sea broken by a few clapboard buildings and the mobile trailer in front of us designated as the office. Dwayne and Sean walked up the trailer stairs as I tried to cover my seeping wound with my T-shirt. The saltwater wind kissed with a jellyfish sting.

Dwayne came out and waved onto the sun-streaked sandlot. From the top of the steps, his arms glided higher than the trailer's roof. "That's it," he called to me, dubiously.

Sean burst from the trailer and jumped in the air to see the campsite. "Wow, look, our new home," he said, surveying the dust.

"Did they say they were hiring?" I asked.

"She said they were taking names. If we live here we'll have a better shot getting a job. But they're not planning on starting up until the strike's resolved. And that might be weeks away," Dwayne said grimly. "I didn't save all winter to be the only black man on an island and be unemployed for a month."

That night I slipped a quarter into the latch of one of the hostel's more obscure doors: you put the coin between the spring-loaded catch and its holster, preventing the lock from engaging even though the door has shut. It didn't take long to find Matt and Dwayne in a bar called the Fo'c's'le. I ordered a Mezcal and a paper towel of ice for my burn and joined them, showing off my great new ID. Proud and quickly drunk, I ambled between their stools and listened to them talk while the bartender hauled a drunk old suit to the curb.

I rolled my ankle over something on the floor. Bending down, I saw a wallet: the drunk's? Matt followed my actions and his blue eyes gleamed.

"Your man left you a little present," Matt said to the bartender, placing the leather on the wooden bar.

The bartender, an oversized load with graying jowls and hoods for eyes, cackled like a jackal finding something to scavenge. "Hey, hey, it's the first of the month! Guy owes me two hundred bucks. How about I take that, and you guys split what's left. Leave me the carcass and don't swipe the cards." He gave us three rounds and we sneaked into the hostel past curfew, up a crisp hundred. I used to feel guilty when I found extra change in pay phones. Here with Dwayne and Matt, I didn't feel any qualms. I thought being a guiltless thief might mean something about becoming a man.

For the next four days, I didn't see much of the guys or the hostel—Tuesday morning I went to a community job meeting and landed day labor, building the foundation of a house on Sunset Way, a mile southeast of Farwest. The wages were decent but the contractor told me straight up he just needed me for the week. That Friday night I got paid and walked to a riverside club with Matt and Dwayne. We danced on the hardwood platform with some young local women—"Women! In Alaska?" Matt yelled happily over "Smoke on the Water." Seafarers flailed to the beat in a cloud of dry ice and a pink-and-blue lights-and-laser show. Dwayne was shadowed by a troupe of groupies, and Matt was closing in on a thin Filipina with a dazzling smile and long shiny straight black hair. In all the excitement, we lost track of the time, had to sneak in my way, and promptly woke up the manager, who promised to kick us out in the morning.

We were evicted bright and early and dragged our bags down to the kiosks by the docks. Sean joined us; he could afford to leave his stuff behind. "Thank the good Lord I ain't old enough to drink," he laughed. Greg consoled us briefly, but his attention quickly turned to the long line of mainlanders in designer shades and fanny packs; the *Pacific Princess* had just docked. Dwayne and Matt debated.

"I'm just thinking about going back to Fresno," Dwayne said. "Scrap this plan altogether."

"C'mon, stay with it," Matt cajoled. "I bet Farwest'll start hiring real soon. And think of the money you'll save without paying lodging!"

"I don't know. That sandlot doesn't look too hospitable."

"Just give it a week. See," Matt pointed toward the bank, "salmon are already starting to spawn. Fishermen ain't gonna let that go to waste for long."

Dwayne contemplated the seagulls circling the confluence of the narrows and the creek. One zoomed into the blue and hastened to the rocks with a flash of silver thrashing from its beak, attracting a flurry of white wings.

I left to order a breakfast corndog near the rainproof hat shop. The weather had been perfect all week: sunny, warm, barely a cloud in the sky, Deer Mountain snow-capped and the sea rich and calm. The cruise-boat tourists had dispersed into the town shops, and Greg ambled toward us, flipping his keys. Those moments without gravity—the plane taking off, the coaster reaching its summit, the still, golden gleam of six keys in the sun—gave me an expectancy of perfection, a feeling that the world was finally tilting into place again. There was no reason to linger. We gathered our things, stuffed ourselves into Greg's bug, and moved on.

Our Tent City shanty took three days to build, and two weeks to really get right. We picked a plum spot between the outhouse and the factory; several other tents were already down, making creative use of cardboard and tarpaulin. Dwayne, Matt, Sean, and I resolved to build the best one around. It was certainly the tallest; Dwayne said he'd only stay if he could stand up without stooping. We started with abandoned pallets from the fishery and made a foundation three 5′x5′ pallets square. Matt and I borrowed Greg's car and stole lumber and plywood from my construction site in the late afternoon. We held a series of evening stakeouts and copped blue plastic tarps covering small boats parked outside a few hillside homes.

We nailed the plywood to the pallets so we'd have a smooth floor, and bolted two-by-fours as corner pillars. Then we ran a second set of pallets vertically along the edges of the foundation. We fashioned scrap wood nine feet in the air as an outline of a roof. Through sheer luck, the front pillars were higher than the rear ones, guaranteeing a run-off for rain. We used cardboard to patch up holes in the sides and covered the top with three overlapping blue tarps.

Susie, Matt's great new girlfriend from the disco, brought in big sheets of clear tarp for our combination window-walls, and her grandfather's old Bunsen burner. Then she took us to the dump to find furniture. We lucked out and scored a pea-green love seat, a chair without legs, and a round wooden coffee table before two black bears spotted us. I grabbed a heavy box of books as we ran back to Susie's car. Inside my find was a dog-eared mix of *Penthouse* and Louis L'Amour. We sectioned the shanty into living and sleeping areas. Our house was so big we could set up our individual tents against the back wall. Sean, who didn't have a tent, elected to sleep on the couch.

We got on the list for Farwest, though the strike still wasn't resolved. "A week, or two, we'll be up and running," said the office woman. "You better be ready."

"We'll be ready," Dwayne grumbled.

The Salmon Capital of the World

At the end of the first week in June, it started to rain. We were fast running out of money, and decided we would share what food we had. I became adept at swiping cans of salmon from tourist traps when the cruise ships came in. Dwayne and Sean went to the library most mornings, and Matt visited Susie. For most of June, we met each other for lunch at the Salvation Army between the docks and the fishery. We waited in a line a quarter of a mile long with striking seafarers, toothless Tlingits, and pregnant teenagers blowing cigarette smoke into their strollers. It was worth it for a free Styrofoam cup of broth and a bologna sandwich. I remember being late one day because it had taken me so long to jerk off to the straight porn in the tent, but Matt saved me a seat.

Using Greg as a liaison, we developed a quick business of showing tourists around in exchange for dinner. Retired married couples and single women were our best customers. We dragged them around and regurgitated tourist materials. Before Louis L'Amour, they'd been our only literature, and we'd pretty much memorized them. We dared our company to ask Ketchikan trivia so we could show off.

How big is this place? *It's the fifth-largest island in the Tongass Narrows, roughly the size of Connecticut. It has been inhabited by Tlingits, a group of Native Americans, for centuries. The island was found by Russian explorers in 1741 and, soon thereafter, named by Spanish adventurers.*

Where the heck are we? *We are about two hundred miles south of Juneau, at the beginning of the Tongass National Forest. In fact, Ketchikan is covered with Sitka pine trees and cedars. Due to the constant bog in any region that averages 155 inches of rain a year, the forests are lined with a soft tussocky muskeg that lightens footfalls.*

What is that big mountain over there? *Well, first let's say that this island is part of an archipelago of oceanic mountains, further carved from the coastline by ancient glaciers. That is Deer Mountain, with its Hershey's kiss summit, which dominates the western shore, where Ketchikan sits.*

The Salmon Capital of the World

Did you say there were Indians here? *Yes. Tlingits hunted, trapped, and fished these lands, mostly undisturbed by other settlers until the late 1800s. The town was named after a Tlingit named Kitschk, who settled along the creek infused by the narrows. Kitcxan refers to "Kitschk's creek," which was Anglicized into Ketchikan during the heady days of the Alaskan Gold Rush at the turn of the last century. Though no gold was ever found in the hills of Revillagigedo, the port city of Ketchikan was recognized by frontier Americans for its abundance of salmon, which return here, in their seventh summers, to spawn and die in the gravelly riverbeds of their conception.*

Why are you guys here anyway? *Ketchikan is sometimes called "Alaska's First City." It's the first port of call for northbound ships. But it is better known as "The Salmon Capital of the World." Ketchikan's economy thrives on seasonal workers who fill the ships and the canneries during the summer. We're seasonal workers and we're hungry and home-less and unemployed because the fishermen are striking. If you feed us cheeseburgers we'll show you where to get the best deals on T-shirts.*

Sean and Matt always made the pitch; Matt liked to do it and Sean didn't, but Sean had a better success rate. More than one motherly soul fell in love with him.

In the next three weeks before we started working, there were three sunny days. The first day, not knowing any better, we went hiking in lichen-bottomed Misty Fjords Park. The ground was a soft and gentle living thing. Spruce trees bathed in a thicket of permafog. ("Don't get me wrong now, it's as pretty as a teenage girl sleeping," cracked Matt. "But no sun for a week, and we go to the rain forest?") The second sunny day, in mid–June, found us sunbathing on the rocks near the water. Matt and Dwayne walked slowly along the bank, giving a scrapped fishing rod a touch-up job and a try. Greg came by to visit, and sat with me while I watched Sean scamper around without a shirt, stub his toe, yell.

"What are you thinking about?" Greg asked me. The thick, salty breeze flipped up flaxen hair that was probably white thirty years ago, when he was a boy. Away from the Starbucks stand, Greg looked frail and jumpy, like a pixie. He said he'd come up from Seattle; Starbucks wanted to know whether they should invest in a Ketchikan franchise, and they were paying for Greg's rental car and apartment.

"How did you meet Matt?" I asked him.

"He ordered a coffee! And he seemed normal. Sort of." Greg smiled. "But what are you *really* thinking about?"

Sean. I stalled. "How nice a day it is? There are more ships today. Maybe that's a good sign." We were silent for a minute. "You know how salmon come back to spawn in the waters of their birth and all that?" Greg nodded. "They come back during their seventh summer, and fertilize the creeks, and then they die. Their olfactory glands lead them back home—their underwater sense of smell tells them where to spawn. But what nobody seems to get," I finished, "is how they know when it's *time.*"

"You look sad," he said gently, and lit a cigarette.

"Maybe. Maybe I've just been reading too many brochures. Can I have one?"

"Sure."

We smoked and watched Sean leap, bare his teeth in a grin, stretch thin arms to the sun.

"What are you thinking about?" I asked him.

"Kind of homesick," he said. "I miss my girlfriend Val. And my brothers. I have two brothers, you know."

"Younger or older?"

"They're younger. I'm thirty-three. Clay's twenty-four and Zack's twenty-six."

"Do they live in Seattle?" I asked.

"Yeah. And do you know the funny thing? They're both gay!" Greg's eyes danced in the sun. "Do you think that's one of those things that runs in the family?"

"I really don't know!" I said.

"You don't have a problem with gay people, do you, Eye?"

I couldn't talk, so shook my head, gazed at Sean. A loon bobbed gently on the waves. We watched the castaway in khaki shorts climb carefully toward us.

"Sean's great, isn't he?" Greg asked softly.

"Yeah," I said. "He really, really is. But all you guys are."

Late afternoon found us in a rock quarry down the bank. We built a fire with tinder sticks and pine cones, baked the cod Matt and Dwayne caught on thin ledges of shale resting over the pit.

The next wave of rain came that night, and it was taking its toll. Our tent was always leaking in one place or another; the best we could hope for was a slow drip. We were all unemployed—it wasn't near dry enough to paint Susie's grandpa's house—and broke. Dwayne's natural tendency toward reflection had turned into moodiness and closely checked despair. Sean was even more withdrawn than usual. When he'd talk, he'd speak darkly of his mother and the residential lock-in where he'd spent the six months after she committed suicide.

Only Matt was really happy, if only for Susie and Louis L'Amour. A former Sonic girl, Susie was a homebody at heart. She brought us to an enormous family banquet one night with bottomless silver tankards of white rice and vast gold vats of crispy lumpias. We were all so hungry then. I supplemented Salvation Army fare by helping myself to the Tatsuda salad bar and eating it on their toilets so I wouldn't have to pay.

On the last sunny day in June, we decided to climb Deer Mountain. I lifted a bottle of red wine from Tatsuda's, hiding it in my jeans leg, and we set out with Sean and Dwayne, who'd found an old basketball somewhere. We played a fast game of horse on a cracked asphalt court in the park. Dwayne nailed every shot he took, it didn't matter where. They didn't even hit the rim.

"Holy fish fry," said Sean, who couldn't hit the narrows from the bank. "You should join the NBA."

"Too old," said Dwayne, swishing another. "I tried. Declared myself for the draft back in '79. Never got picked." Matt shagged his ball, threw it back. "It really burned me to see guys I played with—guys I knew I could beat!—get selected. Guess if I'd gone to UCLA instead of UC-Riverside," he continued, dunking effortlessly. "But that's the way it goes."

Matt, Sean, and I continued up the mountain while Dwayne loped back to camp to write letters. The path took us through a swath of pine, then a pasture of stumps shorn by logging. We traversed over a lateral moraine of rubble and weeds. Finally we hit snow and more trees, and stashed the bottle in a tangle of roots. After two hours, we made it above the tree line and onto a snowy plateau.

"Time for target practice!" Matt exulted. He pulled out an old Magnum. "Anyone want to join me?"

"When did you get that?" I asked him.

"Your man Randy sold it to me. At the hostel." Matt swiveled the gun's chamber, then retrieved, from the pocket of his jeans, a small package of ammunition. He opened it and slid bullets into slots. "Snub nose," he explained. "Go right through the outer layers and explode inside."

"What are we shooting at?" Sean asked.

"Good question. I got a T-shirt underneath my sweats."

Matt pulled off his sweatshirt and then a sleeveless T. He set it on a snowbank and took us fifty feet away, then pulled the safety. "Only brought one round," he said. "Two shots for each of us. Stand back." He held the gun in two hands, straightened his arms, sighted down the barrel, and fired. A tremendous crack rang through the clearing. "Bulls-eye!" he yelled. "Shit. Sucker's got a kick. One more." Another shot rang through the thin clear air. "Think I missed that time." Matt handed the gun to Sean and shook out his right hand. Sean took a lot of time preparing and took two shots that looked like they sailed wide. My turn came. I'd never held a revolver before, and was surprised by its weight. It took two hands to hold it steady. I eyed Matt's shirt between the metal flanges on the barrel and shot. The recoil sent my arms reeling upwards, and my ears wouldn't stop ringing.

"Fuck," said Sean, massaging his slight wrists. "That hurts like hell."

"Good aim, Eye! I think you got it. Take the last one."

I fired again, danced backwards, and handed back the Mag, wishing I could hear anything but echoing powder.

"I think I'm fucking deaf," Sean said. We went to inspect Matt's shirt. There were four small jagged holes, two on each side, like an extra pair of nipples. The brown Hershey's kiss looked steep, pathless, and daunting, and it was already getting late. We decided to descend. Eventually we found our wine and toasted Alaska. Then Matt toasted Susie.

"Susie can shoot," Matt said. "To girls who can shoot!" Sean gulped in laughter.

"You mean, a gun?" I asked.

"No, see. . . . When she has an orgasm, she shoots! Not across the room or anything, but I've seen her juice fly!" He took the bottle from Sean. "Susie's great, but if I had my way, I'd have a harem. I'd have six fourteen-year-old girls at my beck and call." Matt tipped the bottle of snow-cold Merlot into his happy wet mouth.

"I'll drink to that," yelled Sean. "To fourteen-year-old girls!" His laugh caromed gaily off the cliffs.

"To fourteen-year-old baby girls!" Matt yelled back. He passed me the bottle. "Toast?"

To what? To fourteen-year-old boys? To Sean? "To making our way back home before dark," I said.

"Hear, hear!" said Matt, and promptly got us off the path and lost. We wandered in the dusky pines for an hour, steadily heading downhill. West was easy to judge until the sun went down. We reached an overhang, pondered, and leaped off, falling ten feet and rolling another fifty down the hillside. Incredibly, the path rose up to meet us. We got back to find Susie and Dwayne listening to Roxy Music on an old battery-operated boom box her mom had donated for the summer. We spent the rest of the night with Matt's Swiss

Army knife, scraping resin from the chambers of my pipe and smoking it by candlelight.

"I only like female vocalists," Sean quietly announced, around midnight. He snuggled halfway into his sleeping bag and sat crosswise on the love seat, his hands behind his head, against an armrest. I was in the chair without legs. Matt and Sue were in Matt's tent, in a rear corner, and Dwayne was stretched out on the floor, staring at the dark tarp roof. "Ever since she died."

"Do they remind you of her?" I asked him. Sean was silent for a time. I blew out the tea lights on the old stained barrel. I thought he might be crying. I wanted to tell him my mom had died too but I couldn't. Not then, or ever. Maybe I didn't want to show him up. But I thought of her now, on a dig in Mexico so long ago, ecstasy creased on her sunburned face, the stone arrowhead resting between the lines on her palms.

"I don't know," he whispered. Then, more loudly: "Maybe I just like female vocalists, okay?" His voice cracked, but maybe it was just a puberty holdover. He was silent again, and then whispered. "Maybe it's not her I want to be reminded of. She was crazy and depressed so much. She was mentally ill ever since I can remember. So sometimes I think, 'Well, maybe I never really had a mother.'"

Susie or Matt rustled in the corner. Dwayne's eyes were closed, his long body stretching down the floor to the door. I didn't know what to say.

"But there were times when she could take care of me," Sean continued in his grave, careful hush. "More when I was younger. So when I listen to female vocalists maybe that's what it seems like. Like they're taking care of me. And they are taking care of me. With their voices."

"Amen," Dwayne called softly from the planks.

"Or maybe I just want to fuck them," Sean giggled. "Can you turn off the tape? I'm going to sleep."

I punched the switch, then climbed over Dwayne and through the plastic seams. The moon was high and full and I followed it as far as the stony bank. I stood on a tall boulder and peed a platinum rainbow into the sea. I took off all my clothes and threw them on the rocks, then slipped quietly into the narrows. The cold sleek water swirled over me like a dark cape. I wanted to know why she did it. I had an idea until my teeth started chattering and I had to get out. Back in my shorts on the shore, I felt stupid and lonely and home-sick, like a cartoon of a marooned sailor washed ashore on a desert island. But the next morning, when Sean unzipped his sleeping bag, a fresh rush of hope surged through me. His favorite pair of boxers were a wide-legged, brown paisley, torn cleanly in two places along the side seam. They were enough for me to make another tent in my boxers every morning.

Farwest's smokestacks were in fact steaming that morning, a Sunday, as part of a dry run. We started work on the last Tuesday in June. Matt, Dwayne, and I were assigned "filler" jobs midway down line 2. We were given black rubber boots and plastic yellow jackets and pants: slime suits. Our task was to toss salmon parts onto pronged ledges that revolved into the chopper. Further down the machine, the torn flesh was tamped into cans that descended by conveyor from the can loft. By the time they got to us, the fish had been frozen, beheaded, flayed, and eviscerated. They were on their way to tuna-fish-size cans, the likes of which I'd lifted so many times downtown. Sean worked down the line on "cutter" duty, snipping the more prominent skeletal remains from the soon-to-be-sealed products. Behind us, a tremendous tank collected the fish from the eviscerators ("gutters") and held them for us. Sliding the tank's door two inches or so would guarantee a steady influx of oily pink meat; opening it four inches or more sent fish flying all over the floor. Therefore, one rear filler gauged the vertically sliding door and set fish in rows; the two frontliners flipped these fish two-by-two on the rotating ledge, trying to keep up with the whirling prongs.

From the start we worked six days a week, fourteen hours a day. There's nothing to describe but several million cold slick pink sal-mon cuts wiggling their way through my hands, squirting their blood into my eyes. The joints in my fingers were achy and numb every morning and rarely thawed out before lunchtime. We talked and sang songs but I can only remember how much I had to pee, and the long lines for the bathroom, and the difficulty of taking down my yellow pants with frozen fingers. They gave us fifteen-minute breaks every three hours and a half-hour break for lunch. The only time we really got to relax was when someone's arm went through the works and they'd have to close down for an hour. We looked forward, perversely, to these surprise respites. They reminded me of snow days. Dwayne's back was killing him from stooping to the steel tray where we lined up the fish, but he kept on. I'd watch Sean's hair-net bob with the girls down the line and see his scissors flash.

To make up for the lost income of the June strike, Sean and I joined the cleanup crew for four hours each night. We'd hose down the walls and floors and then I'd clean my machine. I got to know every piece of the chopper: the steady prongs, the whirling set of circular razors underneath, the metal rails regulating the cans. A migrant Filipino mechanic who spoke no English taught me how to send the works forward and backward and then left me alone. One evening, about three weeks into my sleep deprivation (by this time, I was averaging twenty hours of work a day), a white girl from Quality Control asked me to try a new cleaner. She said it would be better than just using water. I wondered what difference it made, but gave in. I set the machine on ¾ speed and sprayed the foam on the prongs.

"Is it cleaner?" she asked excitedly, standing back so as not to get sprayed. She was wearing crimson lipstick, a gelled pageboy cut, a clean gray set of cotton overalls, and canvas sneakers, not exactly dressed for the weather in here.

"How should I know?" I asked. I hosed the prongs down. "Should I feel it to see if it squeaks?"

"I guess," she said, flicking her hand to show her indifference. But her face was impatient and expectant, like some major revelation was coming if I would just get on with things.

I felt a prong quickly with my fingers but it slid under me, as oily as ever. I looked back at her and shrugged. "Who knows," I said. "It's always slippery as hell." Just then, I felt a claw pull my left hand. As if in slow motion, I looked back down and told my brain to remove my hand, but it was too late: the machine had taken it. My hand slammed against a metal bar and I was sure I was about to join the Amputee of the Month Club. Then with tremendous, unrelenting force, my wrist bone suddenly caught between a prong and the bar, just before the circling knives. I knew if it broke I was fucked.

"Fuck!" I yelled. "I'm in the fucking machine!" Quality Control girl's face turned as gray as her uniform, and she backed away. I decided I better be really polite and calm otherwise she'd run off. "Hey," I said. "Listen. Please. Could you please *turn the fucking machine off*?" Her eyes filled with tears and she put her hands over her gaping maw. Her backwards pace quickened. "I can show you how," I yelled through my teeth. The pain was intense and I shut my eyes against it. "It's really easy, you just press that button near . . ." When I opened my lids she was running away to the heart of the factory.

She returned with a mechanic who promptly hit the power button. The whirring razor wheels slowly ceased hissing. Great news, but I was still caught in the vise.

"Now what the fuck do I do?" he asked her. She was blank as a chalkboard on the last day of school.

"There's a crank," I said. "If you turn it I can get my hand out."

He jumped at the sound of my voice, having already given me up as another Farwest casualty. In his surprise, he turned the manual wheel still forward, putting even more pressure on my bones.

"You're turning it the wrong way!" I screamed. "Turn it the *other* fucking way!" He did; the prong released, and I lifted my wrist out of line 2. Looking down, I stared at the dime-sized hole all the way to the bone. With my left wrist crooked into my right arm, I wandered back to find Sean. He was walking toward me.

"I heard," he said.

He looked at my eyes, not my wrist.

"Look Sean you can see the bone."

I took a deep breath and held my deformity away from me, as if giving him a present offhandedly, trying hard not to show my affection. It was the only time all summer he looked at me like he cared, but maybe he just felt faint.

"I think you should call an ambulance," he said, and sat with me until it came. My heart swelled up with my hand. The paramedics gave me oxygen and told me I was in shock.

A night doctor stitched me up and gave me ibuprofen, but it only dulled the pain. I got back at five in the morning. Everybody else was asleep. It had started to pour when I was getting stitched up, and rain smacked the tent like bullets. As I tried to get comfortable, the tarp above me collapsed under water pressure onto my tent; then my tent collapsed onto me. Sean gave me the couch and slept on the floor. "When it rains it pours," he slurred over the trickling slurry. Two hours later I reported for work. They sent me to the can loft, where I was supposed to watch a conveyor belt for dented empty cans. I liked it up there. It was hypnotic and warm and the sun bathed the red wooden floor in dusty morning light. During shutdowns we'd sleep like cats in the sunshafts. I had a new game of waving at people using only my left hand, which was three times its normal size.

At lunch I sprinted to the park on Deer Mountain's lowlands and called my dad from a pay phone. I used his calling card; I knew he had planned on visiting my great-aunt Joan in New York. She'd lived in that apartment for forty years, the last twenty without her husband, Herm, and the old penthouse was in disrepair. Dad wanted to help fix it up.

"How are you, dear?" Joan asked. I hoped she wasn't mad I hadn't come.

"Well, I just got my hand caught in a machine and my house fell on me last night, but otherwise things are great!" Sarcasm was lost on my great-aunt, though, who was, anyway, a bit deaf. There was a long silence. "I miss New York," I said lamely.

"That certainly does sound exciting, dear. But Shlomo is out buying extension cords. I don't want you to waste your nickel. I'll tell him to call you back later." Before I could remind her that I was nowhere to be reached, she hung up. I felt hopeless and sure that things couldn't get any worse, until I read the *Ketchikan Daily News* after my afternoon shift and learned that a gay serial killer in Milwaukee had been caught with boys' genitals preserved in his fridge in gefilte fish jars. He'd been picking guys up at bars. I'm not saying it cheered me up. But it gave me perspective. Who knows what could have happened if I'd stayed home that summer? I would have gone home with anyone and taken anything. I took some ibuprofen and slept.

Greg came around and took pity on me, offering to put me up in his place that Saturday night. I happily agreed. He bought two tabs of acid from Blake, a moon-faced kid who'd burned his leg badly on Farwest's incinerator. Greg met me at Tent City that Saturday morning and we drove to a surpassingly beautiful state park on the tip of Revillagigedo, flanked by the narrows and the Pacific. We climbed and smoked and talked and I don't remember a thing besides the peace of high altitude and moss and sea and company and him watching me piss over a cliff.

"I'm sorry," he said. "I didn't mean to stare."

"I really don't care! We're on acid, who cares what you do!"

Greg showed me his dream journal later that night and talked about mysticism until I couldn't take it anymore and flicked on ESPN. In the morning, I took a hot shower and came out in the tight but clean pair of underwear Greg had given me. He smiled approvingly.

"They fit you better than Sean," he said. "He's been up here a couple of nights, too. Beats that ripped-up pair of boxers he's been wearing. Sean crawled out of his blankets in some sorry-looking torn-up rags." Unsure how to take this, I quickly got dressed in yesterday's clothes and said I was ready to go. We drove back to Tent City and I brought my mildewing bag to the laundry building.

The Salmon Capital of the World

Tent City's bathhouse had a dozen coin-operated washers and dryers in the front and long benches great for whiling away the drizzles with Hopalong Cassidy or *Mustang Man*. Since there were no toilets (that's what outhouses are for), sinks took up the middle portion; showers were in the back, sectioned off by gender. There was a rear entrance, and fishermen selling to the factory would sometimes make use of the bathhouse. Once in June, when trying to find an open shower, I'd walked in on two cabin boys, too beautiful to ever remember, sleekly gleaming in modular cells. On this Sunday morning in early August, I started a long-overdue load and read summaries of Ketchikan, scrawled in magic marker by bored launderers on flip-chart pages taped to the cinderblock walls. Each page started with the phrase, "Ketchikan is . . ."

Ketchikan is . . . Alaska's first city.
Ketchikan is . . . beached on Guam by super typhoon Paka.
Ketchikan is . . . built on a trestle over a cliff.
Ketchikan is . . . a breeze.

A Tlingit woman, similarly occupied, struck a conversation with me. She asked if I wanted to get high and took me to her one-woman tent, closer to the narrows. We smoked from a crushed soda can. She told me she was a lesbian.

"That's why I don't mind stripping," she said. "There's no tension for me. See, I strip down at the Marine bar in the off-season. You should come by in September."

I thanked her and said I probably wouldn't be here anymore. We stumbled back to the laundry. Sean was ahead of us, carrying his toiletries and a towel. I moved my clothes to the dryers and checked my face in the mirror, wondering when it was ever going to be time to shave again. I spied Sean's small bag near the sink and had an idea. I slunk to the men's side and called out.

"Sean?" There was no answer. "Yo, Sean, dude."

"What?" he yelled, two cells down. "I'm in the shower."

"Yeah, I figured."

59

Even as the sirens sounded in my head I walked to him because I knew this was going to be my only chance. Naked, his hair streamed back, dripping, his belly shone in rivulets and tributaries and his pubic hair curled over a penis that still seemed to be unfurling, free at last from those exasperating boxers.

"What?" he asked, squinting in the spray. I looked down.

"Just can—can I borrow your razor? I think I want to shave."

"Yeah, go ahead. It's in my bag at the sink. You can just leave it there."

"Okay." I stared at the long brown hairs on his thighs, his small flat ass, committing his body to memory.

"Can you leave me alone? I'm trying to take a shower."

"Oh. Yeah. Sorry."

I tore myself away and down to the dryers, to the next open flip-chart page.

Ketchikan is . . . paying a price for fouling the environment.

Ketchikan is . . . the salmon capital of the world.

Ketchikan is . . . never more than 10 blocks wide.

Ketchikan is . . . rain.

Ketchikan is . . . real Alaska.

"Ketchikan is . . . really sexy," I scribbled, but I think I meant Sean. I ran his sharp steel over my cheeks, mingled his dead cells with mine.

The season was coming to a close. Sean moved to a shanty by the shore that someone had forsaken. One day when he was sick with the flu, I visited him and asked whether he wanted a massage. He refused. "It's kind of like how I am with female vocalists," he joked weakly. He regained his breath and rasped, "I just don't like guys to massage me." He only whispered because he couldn't breathe. He was the first of us to leave. Susie let me borrow her pick-up to drive him to the ferry headed for Bellingham. When he was all packed and saying goodbye to the crew, I rifled through his duffel and took a last reminder.

Sean, from the lock-in in Washington, his dark nipples, torn boxers, our dead mothers, our hug at the ferry. Sean: I took your favorite shirt. It was tie-dyed and bears danced through rainbows. It was too small for me but I thought I deserved it. The pits were the only part that smelled like him and not fish juice. They say you can't take it with you but I hoard these memories like bread in lean winters. I collect them like squirrels stow acorns. I fold them like T-shirts in a bureau and pull them out when I need their small comforts.

I left two weeks later with a cashier's check for four thousand bucks. Dwayne and Matt were staying on until September, when the fishery closed for the off-season. Greg was leaving in October; he drove me back to Gravina, and we promised to keep in touch but never did. I slept the whole way back to Wisconsin. It was nice to be back at home for a bit, even though I understood how much I'd outgrown it. I gave my dad three hundred and fifty bucks for plane fare.

Trance and I met at the beach on the shores of Lake Michigan on the last day of summer. It smelled like the factory: rotting fish guts. The lifeguards were taking down their high chairs and the waves crested with a yellow chemical foam. We waded in a ways together in the cold contaminated lake.

"So you went to freaking Alaska." Trance flipped an old blue Frisbee.

"The last frontier," I agreed.

"The last frontier," he repeated. "Bet that put some hair on your chest."

I turned toward him so he could see. "Look." I pointed to the three brown hairs curling out of my sternum.

Trance looked uncomfortable. "I didn't mean for real," he said. "Fuck, man. I'm never gonna get any."

I looked at his burnished chest, his burgeoning beer belly, and into the hot afternoon haze. "Yeah, well. You're Korean."

Tran flicked the Frisbee over my head. I leaped for it and caught a fistful of air. It soared over the water and landed softly in a school of dead silver fish washed ashore.

Locker Room Chronicles

We all store ourselves away, chain up our lives. Dad and I are storing Mom behind a Master lock. He rents a cage at Your Self Storage Company. It's the cheap alternative to cryogenics. The morning before I go back to art school, we rent a van and lug Mom's clothes and files, her jewelry and her furniture, to the emptied old printing press building across from the health food store. Between the driveway's cobblestones, weeds stretch their stalks to the sun. Sunflowers dance in the breeze before blue-painted bricks. Inside, in Mom's new cage, it's dark and dusty, like a ship's hold. Her partition is lit by a drifting bare bulb dangling from the ceiling, casting for cargo to spotlight. In the box with her swimsuits, a part of me is now imprisoned. With her vacation albums, my memories are locked away. I can't see being her skinny twin, our stick arms the only waves in the Great Salt Lake again. She waded and waded so far but she never went under. Laughing hard, flying kites on the endless clay flats of Puget Sound, swooping like swallows, disallowed. Holding me as a blue-lipped toddler in Playa Azul, after my father pulled me out of the water. She spent her time excavating old cities, and might appreciate more than anyone her life so perfectly preserved now, underground.

My father lets me keep one thing. He leaves the ashes behind, in plastic wrap inside her Matryoshka doll. He has taken a black-and-white photograph of her as a teenager, when he met her in high school in Chicago. You can tell why he fell in love with her. She is a Romanian jazz chanteuse: her highballed cheekbones, the disdainful pout of her lips. I can only recognize her in the photo by her wide, seductive eyes. I fold up a faded lace doily from her vanity table. When I put it over my nose I smell her perfume again, and her sweat, so faintly, whiff of her spirit against the dank inky abandon of her tomb. Dad plans to rent out the house again while he's on sabbatical. He tests the three keys on the lock, hands me one, and leaves to give one to the attendant. I sit in the corner, outside the cage, against the cool oily metal and the damp bricks, watching centipedes and spiders. I swear I won't let go this time. I hold onto the cage when Dad comes back. She would sing in Romanian, on long car rides across the rusty badlands, *This time is not enough.* She'd jitterbug with my father to the scat she could make in her head. My clenched knuckles rattle the metal of her cell to their lost beat. Dad puts his palm against my shaking fist, stills it, and pries my fingertips away.

I try to talk to him in the rent-a-van. He concentrates, sternly surveying the view through the big square side mirror, adjusting its tilt.

"I'm leaving tomorrow," I say. "If it's okay with you I'll take the hatchback."

The cab's bench seat whines to itself, its metal joists absorbing potholes. He has the map out because he has forgotten where the U-Haul place is.

"Dad, I know where it is."

He frowns and folds up the map, precisely, talking to himself.

"Dad?" I reach over to touch him, change my mind, and let my arm stay in the air between us, awkward as a scarecrow.

"Matter does not vanish in black holes," he says. "It exists and so must be ejected somehow. And when it's ejected . . ." he pauses, deliberately lifting the turn signal lever until he is satisfied with its clicking. "When it's propelled back into space, the information is there, but it is, presumably, distorted." He smiles beatifically and waves out his window, into the cerulean sky. "Even so, we may be able to find the history of the universe coming out of these black holes."

We go our separate ways; that afternoon, he leaves the house hurriedly, carrying a briefcase and his gym bag. His squash racket is no longer in the hall. I follow, prowling, to see who he is outside his den. I stake out his gym and sneak in, vaulting over the exit turnstile as soon as there's a line at the entrance. He is not in the echoing caverns, in the squeak and smack, nor the locker room showers, in the soft applause for muscle's silent reign. I make sure. I look each man up and down a few times to get straight. I look myself up and down in the mirror and see him in me—almost imperceptibly, like my mother's teenage picture, another lost phantom.

And I am looking for the boy who slipped away, though any boy will really do, as long as he resembles how I used to look, reminds me how I used to feel. I lost touch. You see. I shake myself away.

What lock does he use? I stare at every one, and at every man undressing, for a flash of familiarity. He is not here in the lockers. Maybe he's in compact shelving. The changing room is a labyrinth of three-walled niches, U's of lockers with a bench in each box, each cubicle facing another. I choose one and change into basketball clothes. Across from me, a boy turns the corner and opens his locker. He looks like Cal used to—blond, a little shorter than me, skinny. He sees me look at him, smiles sheepishly, detaches the safety pin holding the key from his shorts, and unlocks. Then he strips and walks away toward the entrance. I do the same, and follow.

There's a set of group showers off a restroom near the entrance, three poles with five nozzles set evenly apart. The first two are empty but I hear drizzles beyond the wall. I take a deep breath and step around the divider. The blond boy (Tanner pubic hair stage 2/3, genital stage 4/5) grins, turns pink, turns away. I take a spot in the rotation across.

"Can I borrow your soap?" I ask him.

"Are you gay?" he asks, brightly.

"What?" I'm stalling. It's the first thing out of my mouth. "What did you just ask me?"

"From the way you were following me I thought you were," he says sullenly, turning away. "I don't care if you use my soap after I'm done," he says over his soapy shoulder. "I asked you that—" he turns again, holding his penis, "—because I am!"

"You're what?"

"Nothing. You know!"

His hard-on is the angle of each shower's separation, 72 degrees.

"Join the club," he cracks, laughing at his joke. "Everyone is here, practically."

"What do you mean?"

"Nothing. Does your dad work out here or something?" He looks at me hard.

"Sometimes. I mean I think so. Why?"

"Nothing," he smiles again. "Mine does. But he leaves me alone. Anyway, he thinks I'm lifting weights while he swims. Do you want to do anything?"

"I'm just going to take a shower," I say nervously. I am thinking about all the pedophile busts as soon as I got back from Alaska, after the serial killer was apprehended. He'd had this small network of friends who liked boys, like him, who'd liked him before they'd known he was a murderer; and they'd known people, and so on. A hospital administrator overdosed on Dilaudid because of it. I read the papers every day to find Mr. Yuk, but he hasn't shown up yet, even in the local section. "You can do whatever you want," I offer. Meaning, *I'll watch you, if you want to jerk off like the urinal guys at the park.*

Instinctively, he grabs my cock. I clear my throat. He pumps my dick. I am committing a felony and I'm not even breathing. I force the air out:

"I mean, you can do anything you want to *yourself*. I don't care."

He grips once more, hard, and asks, "What do you mean?" Meaning, *Are you sure?*

"I mean, just do you if you want. Do yourself."

"Oh! You want me to do stuff to myself!" He takes his hand reluctantly away from my wobbling penis and resumes slicking over his own.

"So what grade are you?" I ask him, trying to be calm. I am posing because he watches me. I suck in my stomach, flex my biceps, like Arnold at Mr. Universe.

"Eight." He keeps stroking. "Well, going into eighth. My name's Ryan, what's yours?"

"Ivan. I'm a sophomore in college."

"No you're not."

"I am, I swear it. I'm gonna be a sophomore in college!"

"You look like you're only fifteen."

"I'm twenty."

"Cool. Then *I'm* fifteen." He rubs his hands together in a lather, suds his penis with foam. It looks like an eel coming out of the lake. "Are you *ever* gonna do anything with me?" He looks longingly, downcast. His preternaturally blue eyes are slit with the pouty consternation of unanticipated challenge. Close up, he is a dove, pale and downy, he is trying to be nonchalant, and we both laugh from being anxious.

"You're too young," I shrug. "You have to get older."

"I'm sixteen!" he says, mad.

"You have to get older."

"Fine! I'm seventeen!"

"It doesn't happen that fast." But maybe it *does*, I think, wildly— maybe Dad solved the disintegrity of time after all, right here in the men's locker room at the college rec center.

The boy's face flushes a deep pink. "Nobody else even cares!" he shouts. "Nobody's going to know! We're the only ones here! Nobody even *uses* these showers!"

"Shhh," I tell him, and touch the soap on his chest, rub it in. He eyes my hand like it's a mosquito, as if there's no reason to bother just touching him *there*.

"I did something with an old guy here once," he says, trying a new tack. "But he was really big. Are you hard?"

"About half."

"Did you ever measure yourself?"

"No. Well, sometimes. It's like, seven."

"Cool," he smiles, and jerks harder. "Do you come here a lot?"

"No. I leave for school tomorrow anyway. In Pennsylvania."

"Just this once then," he breathes into my ear. "Just pop a boner. Just do something with me this once."

I have to but I can't.

"Just pop a boner. I have to go soon. Just pop a boner. Just let me suck it, just this once, just for a little bit. Look, I'm pre-cumming!" He wipes his hand on his Dove.

"I'm scared," I say. That part is true. "I don't think I should. You giving me a blowjob is the same as me raping you."

"That's the stupidest thing I've ever heard," he says, and glares in disbelief, like I just kicked him in the nuts for the fun of it. He cranks his shower off, whirls and tugs his towel over his cock, binding it against his stomach. When he gets to the divider, he turns again and mutters, "You can keep the soap." The thinning stick has glued itself to the metal ring around the pole. I unstick and slide the glabrous bar around my neck until it deliquesces. It streams across the white-lyed grout between the pale blue tiles and whirlpools down the drain.

Outside, late summer sun casts innocence over the sleepy hills. The cicadas are thrumming violas and a scarlet tanager whistles through an air pocket on its way back to the aviary. The gym doors are curiously open to the well-swept, curving sidewalk, and I reconsider. Maybe I should go back and tell him I changed my mind? Hey Ryan, I made a mistake. I was surprised and confused. I've been lonely for so long. I'll drop out of school and be your boyfriend. I don't care how old you are. I understand: your desire: your intensity. I understand the way your blood flows. I feel your pulse. I see you. Meet me in the last toilet stall, I'll leave the door unlocked.

Back inside, now in the field house, the air is thick as thunder clouds, the precipitation of kids bumping and grinding. A zebra races down the sideline and brays at the players, tweets three times with the silver dangling from his lips. Parents are cheering and screaming, and balls drum their beat onto the rubberized red flooring. I slink behind the courts to the far wall, check out Argentina versus Illinois, Canada versus Spain, Romania versus Puerto Rico, white and blue, red and yellow, green and black. It's an age-group tournament from the looks of it: everybody seems to be fourteen or fifteen.

A couple of guys on the Puerto Rican squad are cute, but too tough for me. The Romanian kids are more slender—or half-starved—and more refined. Mom's ancestors, Jews and gypsies, came from Bucharest in 1900, just as the pogroms swept Russia. They're losing, huddling with their coach. I check the portable scoreboard, wonder what it would be like to live there, wonder if I would I chase myself anymore, wonder if I still turn myself on. *Hey Ryan,* I try out in my head, *I changed my mind, do you still want to, do you still have time?* My legs are shaking so hard I have to sit and hold my knees down with my hands. I pretend I'm just stretching.

Boys sweat and collide, yelling and clawing. A Rockford reserve covers up his skin-and-ribs torso with his uniform; a Puerto Rican shooter nails a jumper; a curly-haired Romanian gets knocked down. The coach pulls him from the action.

I trail the boy's limp to the bubbler, scope appendages: long, tan, scrawny, ideal. I don't know what I am. I think I need to be a medic but I settle on sports trainer.

"What's happening, man?" I ask the boy. When he looks up water dribbles into the cleft in his chin.

"We're losing," he replies. His high voice gives an airy element to his muddy enunciation.

"Are you okay?" I take a drink.

"Huh? Yeah, a little bit hurt."

"I'm training to be a sports doctor," I blurt. *I changed my mind,* I think. My presidential smile covers my lie. "I'll check it out for you, if you want."

The boy looks at me oddly, as if he doesn't get it. I lilt my lips, as sweetly as I can muster, arch my eyebrows.

"Okay, I guess," says the boy. "Let me tell my coach."

And he scrams. A whistle blows forever, not for any egregious violation, but for the end of the kid's game.

I hustle out to the quadrangle that conjoins the outdoor courts and sand volleyball pit to the dorms, so I can deftly intercept the youth before he changes, before I change my mind again. In my head, I catalogue the dorm rooms of university friends. The showers are in the rooms, most of them. The crows circle in slow motion, scanning for any windbucked foundling abandoned outside the Audubon reserve. I hope they don't attack the tanager. Near the volleyball pit, I pretend to relax by a maple tree, work on stilling myself. The Romanian boy, with his guileless face and his brown curly hair, is walled by a gaggle of chattering teammates, walking my way.

The boy sees me, stalls. He falls from his group and sizes me up. He looks a little like that old picture of Mom.

"You ready?" I ask. "It'll take five minutes. What's your name?"

"Aleksandr."

"Ivan. Nice to meet you. Good game."

The boy shrugs. His limp's walked off. Aleksandr's teammates leave their small forward in my detention. In passing, I salute the coach.

"The doctor," clarifies Aleksandr. Coach waves.

My plan is, loosely, this: go up to his room, ask him to shower.

Have him lie on the bed face down, towel over his butt. My hands will heal him. Aleksandr will get hard. I'll turn him over. His cute Russian roommate will come in. They'll laugh at each other and have nervous and unbelievably erotic sex. Then I'll go see if the blond kid's still hanging around the locker room. I am waiting until the other players go upstairs, so as not to arouse suspicion.

You got some shit to ponder . . .

"Where should we do it?" asks Aleksandr. "You can come up to my room, if you want."

"I don't know . . ." I trail off, watching his cadre file safely inside. I'm thinking of the clerks at the dorms by the main entrance and it occurs to me how easily we can circumvent them; we can take the elevator all the way up from the parking garage, the dorm's foundation, one level underground.

"C'mere a sec." I wag my finger to coax Aleksandr into a dark concrete alcove and then down garage stairs. "I know another way."

Around the corner, my eyes adjusting to the dim underground, I spy the outline of a dingy abandoned mattress shoved into another stairwell. As soon as I sense this one blind opportunity, my game gets away. The rules I've abided by since I read those Dutch sex studies trickle right down the stairs, past a scuzzy throwaway bed in a parking garage. I changed my mind—I am trying to convince myself. I changed my mind. I *want* to now, remember?

The task is set. "Lie down on that."

It's almost black in here, empty but for two badly parked cars. Aleksandr looks unsettled, but he does it anyway.

"Where does it hurt?" I ask, by the book.

He points to his side, above his shorts.

"Take off your shirt."

"Why?"

"So I can see it. What happened?" I turn away from my own toothsome smile. "You get elbowed?"

"Yeah. But I'm all right. I don't know why you ask me to take off my shirt." Nevertheless, he does, twisting it between his fists.

And now, I think again, we could go upstairs—but it has to be over and done with. Paranoia creeps along the tracers of car lights. Security could be right around the corner. We have to do this fast. I'm so close. I admire his chest, the way his sternum almost pokes through like a nascent wisdom tooth. I feel the bruise, red and splotchy, but plainly superficial.

"Yeah, you'll be okay. Let me massage it for a sec?"

Do you wanna go to my place Aleksandr? You're really cool and fine and stuff. Come to my house, and I can look at you in your uniform, and give you a massage, just like this morning when my eyes were still closed, like every dream I won't confess. Don't worry, my dad won't even notice that we're there.

I drift my fingers along his taut skin, examine Aleksandr's soft brown eyes, and find detachment, traps, escape, dispassion. I skirt my thumb a millimeter under the fraying elastic of his pale blue briefs. It can all be within my grasp, if I just drop and close my hand. He doesn't want me to. I change my mind.

The band releases—why? why?—snapping back, vibrating through me like a shotgun's kick; Aleksandr stands up, balls up his shirt in one hand, backpedals. I steal over, shadowing, and massage naked shoulders in the dark parking garage.

The kid's all bones.

Twenty seconds complete our retraction. We sprawl outside in disarray, legs adjusting back to life, as if we'd been lying down in a tent for five days high on K2, waiting out a storm; as if we'd been buried alive.

"Want to check out—the sauna with me—inside—below the courts?" I invite him half-heartedly, terse and wooden as a ventriloquist's dummy, as if some jerk's jerking my vocal chords in and out, slapping my back for affirmation.

"No, I have to get back." His eyes are wide. The hand not holding the shirt is quivering. "See you," he says, with a wavering finality.

The boy races up the dormitory stairs, and it hasn't at all gone as it was supposed to, the thousand times I've fantasized this chance.

Locker Room Chronicles

I pick up a lonely basketball someone has forgotten in the weeds, take a few shots on the empty outdoor courts, and head back to the gym, cradling the orange globe like a stray kitten I have pledged to protect. Mechanically, I limn the sidelines of the tournament and take the back stairs down. I turn the ball in to the lost and found, half-expecting to see myself among the cufflinks and crutches and work shirts spending the rest of their lives in a corner of the equipment room. Just then, Ryan lopes out of the locker room. He pretends not to see me as he turns his key in. I turn, step in front of him, and bump his chest with my shoulder as he tries to get past.

"I changed my mind," I tell him. "If you still . . ."

He rolls his eyes, cracks a grin, puts a finger to his lips. Meaning, *Careful.* From the locker room, a tall thin bearded man walks out and up to Ryan. "My dad," Ryan mouths, and sticks out his tongue. They walk down the hallway together. I watch them go, and Ryan waves discreetly back, once, light and unmistakable.

In my old niche, I untie my shoes. Two men in street clothes have followed me, one after the other. They circle independently, like planets around a sun or cars in the Indy 500, rotating through the locker room. When they come back to my U I take off one more thing. Laps two and three: a sock here, a shoe there. I take care to fold my shirt and pants, dispersing them evenly along the bench. On the fifth lap, I pull down my underwear and wave it. Yellow is the caution flag but my white briefs mean surrender. I swivel on the bench to face the lockers, so they can see my ass this time. On lap six, I turn around again to face their orbit and place the towel Indian-style over my genitals, so my followers can only see a fringe of pubic hair, my solar flare.

They stare. I look at the tiles. I harden underneath the terry cloth. On revolution seven, my penis is a towel rod, jutting into space. The atmosphere must be sizzling, because Planet 1 seems to have burned off. Planet 2, a beefy football type, whirls back and stops to look. His revolutions are happening faster and faster. Soon he will be fixed, magnetized for good. I reposition myself so he can see my profile, the angles of my nose and elbows and boner. I only feel too exposed in his absence. Some observers can see me, and some cannot at all. I must gain control over this visibility. I roll the towel to the edge of my penis, twitch it up and down. On lap eight, the weightlifter waggles his thick neck to gesture me outside. I pretend I don't see him.

I grab my towel and go to the scale in the last locker row. Three naked men with wet bald domes appear immediately behind me. I hand my towel to one of them; another adjusts the silver weight so that the cantilever's in the middle of the box; and the third watches, smiling. They are all my father's age. They're part of the medical school, I hope, because I am the boy on the scale.

"One-fifty-one and a quarter," pronounces the calibrator. His index finger lightly taps still the pendulous tapered head of the metal counterweight.

"You're in good shape," encourages the man with empty hands. He points to his beer belly and guffaws, and I laugh even though I'm supposed to be voiceless, marble. Unreal. I pad to the showers, the ones that people use, by the pool. In this open room are six poles. I take the one in the near corner. There is a sagging white man in the middle; in the far corner is a beautiful black collegiate. My eyes are closed to leftover shampoo, the stinging anti-dandruff kind my father uses. I am sure he was here. I clean every body part, intently languid; I make the shower hotter every time my skin gets used to it. I want it just short of scalding. The man in the middle looks at me, then back at the athlete's ass in the other corner. He tracks between us like he's watching a tennis match. Ivan Lendl v. Yannick Noah in the rec center court showers. He turns to show me he's masturbating, but I don't really care. This might have been exciting but it suddenly seems sad.

The sauna is a slatted pit of glowing coals. I try to sit on the bench without a towel and leap up, a live fish thrown on a grill plank. I think I gave my sac a third-degree burn. Finally situated, only the balls of my feet on the wood, I look out the small plastic window to the drying anteroom, then watch the sweat bead in my pits and reach critical mass, rolling in slow tickles down my side. Slitting my eyes to the heat, I feel the cool draft of the opening and closing door. A man in a towel stands over me, stoops to take a closer look. I tip back onto my elbows until my back hits the next bench, startle forward, flex my stomach to recline. I feel his breath on my penis.

"I see you like I see the sun in the morning," he says, breathlessly. His right arm is yanking up and down. "Muscles straining! Gift from heaven!" He gasps and is quiet.

I can't respond. I am only here for his eyes. The wind again in the cave, and sooner or later all my followers are here: the two planets, the three doctors at the scale, the man in the middle of the showers, the guy who thinks I am the sun. They put their towels on the floor and kneel in front of me silently as if waiting for a sign from a dying mistaken hero on a dais. I wonder if they are facing Mecca. I cannot hold this position any longer. My Achilles are frying on the wood. Men part for me like the Red Sea and I go to the steam room.

In here it's Bergen-Belsen. The fog pumps from the ceiling so you can't breathe or really see. There are shapes on top of each other in the corner. When my eyes adjust to the mists, I configure two men having sex on the slippery benches: the athletic young guy from the showers is mating with a balding man from behind, slapping his ass every third stroke.

"How bout this shit, Professor?" He sounds like he means it. "How about this shit? Don't fail me now!" he laughs with great white teeth.

All Professor can do is grunt. I slide down the bench. He can't see me. His eyes are closed above his cougar nose. He looks at and then through me, into the adsorbate. His expression is a fierce grimace, a rictus of painful happiness. It's the tortured look my dad gets halfway into his last chin-up, veins in his forehead bulging, just before gratification.

"Company?" squints Professor. He's not Dad, after all.

"Hey little fella," the fucker acknowledges. "Wanna be next?"

I shake my head. When I get outside I feel like I just tanked a final, like I answered every question wrong.

Prisoners of War

D ad was less withdrawn than usual as I packed that evening, but I couldn't look at him. I was guilty of everything. I tried hard not to talk. He gave me fifty bucks for luck. Soon he would go to the Black Forest, he said, to study the rotations of twin stars. He called them doppelgangers. His voice rose and bounced around his study as I hung from the bar, playing pendulum. I'd swing just far enough so the wood on the transom cut into my wrists. He joked that he'd be marking trees with ribbons as he made his way to work. He looked forward to blood sausage. I thought he was just happy we were leaving.

The drive to Philadelphia was long and would have been dull, but I was entranced thinking of its twinkling anomie, the lights like a circuit board under the night sky. I'd made the mistake of packing everything I ever wanted to see again. The night before I'd had a premonition that one of us would be leaving forever. I had to open the windows to breathe. I tried to look back but the rearview only showed my possessions. A mattress, a pillow, my books. A lacquered Chinese tin that my mother used to put cookies in before they got cold. She said that it sealed the moisture in, but the lid was never airtight, and they always got crumbly. Pieces kept breaking off the whole until there was nothing left. There was still a rind of crumbs limning the corners of the square gold bottom. It hadn't been washed in six years. I brought it along thinking it would be a good place to keep drugs.

Chicago was a mess. A DJ said that a truckload of fish had fallen from the back of a truck and splayed all down the highway. She played the Smiths as I jerked down the Dan Ryan: *Punctured bicycle, on a hillside, desolate. Will nature make a man of me yet?* Gary, Indiana, was a grid of rusty refinery exoskeletons and electrical massifs crowding together on the lakeshore like mutated flamingos. The water looked black and oily from the bridge. At four in the afternoon I got a flat tire, and some guy named Ed took me to a repair shop somewhere in flat, rainy Ohio, where I was taken in turn for Dad's cash. I got a paranoid feeling that this was all pre-arranged, but it might have been Trance's speed, which I'd snorted at a rest-stop near Toledo. It went in like needles.

At seven I was bumping through Appalachian tunnels, listening to Bible call-in shows that clarified the link between heresy and AIDS. "God hates fags. God kills fags. Any questions? Punch in G-O-D-R-O-C-K on your touch-tone phone to talk." By eleven I was punching open another capsule in a stall at a turnpike Roy Rogers. I stood at the urinals for five minutes, dangling bait, but not one trucker bit. By one-thirty the next morning my junk was back at school. I didn't know what I was doing there. I wasn't an artist but I wasn't much of anything else either. I liked to read and look at pictures. The school had integrated some of its housing with neighborhood apartments. I was staying at 16th and Lombard, right off South Street. There was absolutely nowhere to park.

Center City Philadelphia was a cramped and narrow grid of one-way streets designed to confuse and infuriate. Circling the block meant driving at least six blocks out of your way. Either Lombard was off my beaten path before, or there had been some sort of change over the summer, or I only noticed it motoring through the gloaming, but it was clear that the streets were now being patrolled by extraordinarily tall and busty black women in miniskirts. I pulled into an alley off 13th Street to ask directions, and one of the throng clacked up to my window.

"You need something baby?" she asked in husky timbre.

"I'm just looking for Lombard again." I looked at the grime of my dashboard, sneeze sprays and soda stains and fingernails I'd chewed and spewed.

"Honey, those girls up there ain't no better than me. You need some head babydoll? You a student?" I nodded. "I'll give you student discount. Twenty dollars and for you baby, I'll swallow."

It had started to drizzle. Glamorous dashes of copper glistened from the lamp-lit rain, electrifying the fortified cobblestone in Camac Alley. From an awning up the street a searchlight illuminated and froze my windshield's insect cemetery. My street concierge blanched. "Lombard's two blocks that way," she said, pointing left, and hustled off around the corner.

I spent the night moving into my box studio: third floor, two windows, kitchen and bathroom carved away from the rectangle, a white wooden loft bed taking up half the space. The windows opened onto Lombard. I fell asleep to hoots and catcalls.

The next afternoon the call number that I'd known by rote since the age of sixteen—612.661—was like a mantra in my brain. I had to have it. I continued my quest at a nearby all-women's school with reciprocal library privileges. My stereo was tuned to Jazz 90, and my open window let in clean Delaware Valley air. I bought a package of Ganesh beedees at an Indian food store on my way out of town along Lancaster Avenue, the straight line of row houses disintegrating block by block until you reach the obsessively tended burbs: Merion, Wynnewood, Haverford, Bryn Mawr. Beedees are truncated cigarettes, unfiltered and rolled with a tobacco leaf; they look like dollhouse cigars and have a sweet, pungent aroma. I glided the automatic gearshift into neutral as I made a move to turn, squeezed the steering wheel in place between my knees as I lit a match and inflamed another beedee, held to my lips by its thin pink thread.

An ocher sun choked through low clouds, and tower bells were tantric, chanting six o'clock. I didn't know my way that well but I had a good map, so I navigated toward the psychology library. I acknowledged nobody. Anonymity made me unseen. I knew the routine. At the psych building, I tried the front door—locked. I walked around the gray, two-story stone building, for the back door, which the legs of a chair held ajar. I scoured vacant corridors. There was a wing in back, housing the stacks. The lights were off. I tested the glass door: it was open. I looked around and was alone. Dr. Stolz, Dr. Stolz, let down your hair.

I flicked on one column of fluorescent lights, followed the arcane racking system until I hit the 600 section. My fingers raced along the bindings, up one shelf, down one more, a scamper through the castle. Finally, not in their place, but further down the row, were Herbert and Lois. Nobody had beaten me to them. I riffled through the pages, making sure they were mostly there, wondered if the dykes would miss them, guessed not, and purloined the family jewels.

I scampered out the door, thinking, What an easy theft. I felt the breeze and the peace outside, the wind whipping up my shorts; and was distinct, whole, gazing above the tree line at the pale, failing sun.

Taking no chances, I placed the simple navy hardcover under the passenger seat and headed back to my apartment. I had a project in mind: reproducing medical photos of nude boys whose faces were already censored. I needed to figure out ways to censor their loins. I thought I might bring two or three boys together into one print and cover their genitals with cutouts of photocopied hands. I always liked Xeroxes of body parts. When you set machines on high contrast the parts look three-dimensional because the outline is so thick with toner. They were the bas relief of chalk around dead bodies in the street.

Back in the city, I pulled into an Amoco kitty-corner from my pad. I scrounged change from my pocket and picked up a shiny lime-colored bag of something crunchy and toxic. On my way back to the car, I yanked a free paper from a black box by a streetlamp that had just started shining. The banner headline said, *Au Courant*.

Upstairs, I fell upon the sloping carpet, dropped the book and newspaper beside me. I left the television and lights off. I was hoping to make this last as long as possible. I slowly opened the front cover to a photo of the backside of a naked boy on a scale. I knew that picture; it had been reprinted in *Growth Diagnosis*, a book I had studied and vandalized at sixteen.

I peeked again at the blonde's high, rounded butt cheeks, and at Dr. Herbert Stolz by the scale, looking solemnly down to where his patient's young penis would be. I couldn't help myself. I began to rub the satiny skin on the inside of my wrist through my zipper.

It was the situation: boy, doctor, exam. I could've jerked off for days on that number. As I shook and splattered, I was thinking, What does this kid look like on the other side? Is he as hard as I am? Did he ever imagine people would be jacking off to his picture? Did Stolz show him how to stroke it? Nothing's ever turned me on as much as vulnerability, consciously exposed.

In my post-orgasmic trance, I climbed out the window of my efficiency and dropped to the twilit fire escape with my newspaper. The *Au Courant* was exciting enough to seem taboo; it was the first gay periodical I'd ever read. I was drawn to Help Wanted listings— escorts / strippers / massage. I ripped out one with the word "discreet" and felt myself up for a quarter.

A split-second of consideration and I was skittering toward asphalt glittering with post-consumer pennies, shattered crack vials, bottle caps and condom wrappers, street kids sauntering from the parking lots to 16th. The torn clipping was in one hand and a beedee in the other; I power-walked two blocks to the corner with the pay phone that the art students and the prostitutes were always fighting over. It was free at last, thank God almighty, so I sprinted across the street, slotted a coin, and read again the ad in my hand.

As I wondered why I was doing this, the dial tone interrupted. I punched in the number and let it ring. My heart slammed into my mouth as a voice came on, but it was only the machine. *Well, give it a shot, Eye, can't hurt—*

"Hi, my name's Ivan," I stammered and took two deep breaths, willed my pulse to slow. "I'm a student. Your ad said you were looking for . . . employees?" A man came on the line before I could think what else to say. *Lord help me I am in!*

"A student?" said an ingratiatingly nasal voice. "I'm Don. You want to work? I run this whole fucking thing so you're talking to the right man."

"Yeah, I do, I want to . . ." Two tall girls in miniskirts and precipice pumps giggled by the brick wall behind the booth. "To join your organization," I wavered.

"I see. Have you had any experience?"

"Uh—a little—"

"What have you done, exactly?"

"I'm on a pay phone. They're plugging in my phone line next week. See, I just moved down to Center City."

"Oh, I gotcha. Well. What are your physical characteristics?"

"I'm six feet, one fifty-five, athletic, I used to play soccer in high school."

"Wonderful. Why don't you get back to me in a couple of days?"

I don't have that much time. I'll change my—"Let's meet tonight, is that cool? Can we see each other this evening?" I asked, trying to sound refined and not desperate, but not fooling anyone.

"You make it here, kid, if you want to so bad."

"You won't be sorry, I promise."

"All right, we'll talk later. Be at 8th and Colfax at 8:30."

"Sure." Colfax. I knew it from taking wrong turns, it was just past South.

"Look for a big guy, actual fucking bodybuilder weightlifter type, his name's Craig. Who do you wanna say'll meet him?"

"Huh? Me, Ivan."

"In other words, *Ivan,* what name do you wanna use?" I wasn't sure if he was being snide because of me or if that was just the way he talked.

"Oh . . . call me—Eye—or, I mean, Jeremy." It just came into my head.

"Jeremy?"

"Yeah." I hung up and left, disdainful of the street queens who were starting to make fun of me. My mind was on my future and I studied my walk in the new glass lobby of my old Institute dorm as I crossed Spruce. It was bouncy and confident, like I just aced a pop quiz.

Spinning under the scaffolding, I considered how to prepare for this meeting. First thing, I'd have to smoke a joint so the whole idea didn't seem so nuts. Running my palm over my chin, I decided to shave to look younger. *Going from chicken to wolf. . .* I asked myself if this was going to work out, if I was going to be attracted to these guys, and decided, I don't care, I can fake it.

Home: an iron railing, stone steps, front door, two flights of stairs, my efficiency, 3-F. I felt the velvet of my newly smooth face, *now drop and give me fifty—it'll make your chest look bigger.* I placed my first gay paper, stripped of the clipping, underneath the bathroom sink and took a warm shower, leaving the door open to defog the mirror. My body fully lathered, I rinsed my hair and stepped out. The floor was all wet. I needed a curtain and a bath mat. *With what money, kiddo,* my mom always said when she couldn't buy something she wanted.

The mirror slanted down, framing my hair and my knees. My hands foamed bubbles so they covered the fresh down between my pecs. I picked up the razor; decided against it; then chose to lift most of the hair under my navel instead. I firmed my body, posed, turned around. Watching blood thicken, I didn't think I'd ever seen my eyes so open and so free.

I checked my watch and the speed-metal drummer rattled the cage in my chest. Very soon something inside me was going to give. The ropes were fraying. The imminence of certain change impelled me to cinch my baggy paint-stained Levis with a rope from my hatchback. I threw on a pink oxford shirt, left it unbuttoned; it was still muggy outside. Keys, wallet, fake ID, no reason to take my glasses. They'd make me look older and I wanted to trust my night vision.

It was a twenty minute walk to 8th and Colfax: down 16th past South, a left on Mole, past the ladies of the twilight, who turned smaller and less busty and glitzy the further west I wandered. On Mole the crack dealers gave their pitches and then left me alone. "I'm cool," I kept saying. "I'm cool." The row houses, mostly two-story brick, were a mix of family homes and crack houses, shooting galleries and makeshift shelters, rotting weed-crazed plots of boarded blight. Either it was windy or my hands were shaking, because it took half a matchbook to fire up a Lucky Strike. Under a street lamp, unfiltered smoke settled into clouds between me and a sliver of moon. I tapped my Lucky compulsively and loosed its cherry to gravity, letting it smolder into the sidewalk, then impatiently stamping it out. Where the fuck was he?

"Craig," I said to the street lamp.

"Jeremy," shouted someone. It didn't sound as deep as a bodybuilder should and I almost forgot my pseudonym. "Jeremy? Are you Jeremy?" the voice asked from close by.

"I'm him," I told the shadows. "You must be . . . ?"

"Craig." A beefy white guy with a Phillies cap and goatee materialized beside me. "Let's get you back to the house. We're about a block away. I didn't think it was you when I was walking up here. You're very young."

"Do you know how old I am?"

"No, Don didn't tell me. He said you were a student but he didn't say high school. It's cool, that's what some of these guys want anyway, smooth bodies, you know? Just don't get us in trouble," Craig winked.

"Sure." He seemed so calm. My adrenaline, meanwhile, was approaching heart attack level. "Believe it or not, I just turned twenty."

"You're kidding me. You look about fourteen with that shirt open like that. You could absolutely pass for sixteen. They're growing up faster and faster these days, you know. . . . Short walk, hey? Here we are already."

We approached a neck-high iron gate. Craig buzzed the intercom. "It's us, Don." The lock popped and we stepped down a walk to a small apartment building.

"Welcome to my house," he said.

"Does he—does that guy live with you?"

"Who, Don?" I nodded. Craig laughed. "Hell, no! I work for him. This is his office. He gives me a good deal on rent. Trust me, I'm not with Don for any other reason." Craig rang a doorbell for the first floor, under the awning of an upper landing.

"Come on, come in, get your asses inside, are you both here?" asked a familiar nasal voice from behind the newly open crack.

Craig stood between us, my eclipse.

"No trouble finding him," he said, ushering me into a small kitchen across from a stairway. "For a second I thought we were illegal: he looks real young." Craig moved away to display me. "Jeremy, meet Don."

Don was a bag of bones with a potbelly, his dour expression accentuated by a thin mustache. His hair was slicked back, combed over what was probably a bald spot. Underneath his leather jacket, he wore a wife-beater tucked into his black jeans.

"Nice to meet you. I appreciate the short notice thing."

"No problem," Don rasped. "Usually I want to give guys some time to think before they get themselves into this. You," he hissed, "look great. I'm interviewing two other guys right now. Make yourself comfy."

Don led me into a small, square living room. There were two faded couches, a few mismatched chairs, a dresser in the corner near the bathroom door, and a large television. The other potentials sat one to a love seat, ignoring each other in favor of more slickly produced unsolved mysteries on the blue box. I sat on the floor. Don began the official greetings:

"Let's get this shit going. Why don't we go around and you can tell us a little about yourselves." He pointed to the swarthy man on one couch as Craig left for the kitchen.

"I'm Al," the man gulped. His voice cracked. He cleared his throat and braved on. "I'm twenty-four and I've come here before, so I know you and Craig."

"Al worked with us for a month or so," Don informed the room. "Whaddaya, all ready to come back?"

"I feel ready, Don. I've thought about it, and I'd like to do it again."

"Take off your shirt, Al. You're gonna have to anyway."

Craig lumbered upstairs, a six-pack under his arm.

Al hesitated. "All right. I've been working out—not as much as I'd like—it's expensive." He took off his T-shirt. Fluffy dark hair sprouted from his wide shoulders. Tony was more soft and squishy than stocky.

"You obviously haven't worked enough," Don remarked. "Ever hear of sit-ups?" (Not that he was one to talk.) "Craig up there has the same weight, betcha he's got even more than you, but it's been converted to fucking muscle, so it works. You know the numbers. What do you think it should be?" he hollered upstairs. "One eighty-five, tops?" Craig was silent. "Get back to us when you're there. We'll put you to work then."

Al's eyes flared in terrible surprise. He sat silently in turmoil, then stood and stared us all down one by one until he got to Don. "If I'm not calling, I've found a spot with someone else."

"Oh, sure. Go to Metro Men; they'll take you for a ride." Don waved imperiously to the door. Al grabbed his shirt back and stalked off. Relieved and not sure why, I glanced at the other boy. He was skinny and pallid, handsome in a sickly way, like a wounded soldier. His thin smirk captured the extremist hauteur of the justly condemned. It made me feel like a P.O.W.

"At least I treat you guys honest." Don looked us over. "Well, it had to be done." He unfolded a director's chair between us, sat erect, and opened a notebook, relished a quick pen stroke across a page. "That's it for Al," Don called up to Craig. "Don't let him sneak back in. I'm not running a goddamn burlesque show." He tipped his prescription shades down his nose, leering. "Although you boys probably wouldn't know nothing about those. I remember when I was your age."

We stared blankly back at him.

"Oh well, that's it, that's the fucking agenda tonight, weeding out the guys who won't do the job." Don turned to my compatriot. "You're Jeff—no—Jesse—right?"

"Doesn't matter," shrugged the kid. "I'm eighteen. I'm here because—"

"I don't need to know why, dear. I need to know how. Experience?"

"Plenty of sexual experience."

"Okay. Good. Take off your shirt."

The boy discarded a dull white waiters' dress shirt. His chest was small, hirsute, curving over his ribs so that his skin looked hollowed, like the hide had been taken off someone else before he got it. His body had the hue of Mom's cremated remains.

"Fine," Don said. "Got a better name than Jesse?"

"Oooh . . . maybe Tracy?"

"What about Trip?" Don fired back.

"Ashley?" suggested Craig from above, the word of God.

"That fine?" Don regarded Jesse, who nodded quickly, happy. "Ashley it is. OK? You might want to think about shaving before appointments. Next?"

"I'm Eye," I said, forgetting myself. The phone rang. Don picked up, moving to the couch Al had vacated. He lurched over the side to grab an appointment book and motioned wildly to Craig's balcony.

"Rolodex?" Craig boomed down. Don nodded vigorously. "Down there, on the TV stand. Ashley can you hand Don that—"

Ashley rolled his eyes, rose laconically, and fetched the files. Don grabbed them and panted into the phone.

"Hello?" Don grunted. "Speaking. Don't mention it. We aim to please." His gruff, guarded tone became dulcet, serviceable. He rubbed his hands together, cocking his head to view a card, crooking his neck to hold the phone. "Date and time?" He eyed Ashley, then me. "Look, Chas, Ted's no longer available." He held the phone away from his ear. "He's dead to me, Chas. Find him on your own." Don batted his lashes at Ashley, who looked away. "Here's the deal, you leave right now, you get two for the price of one. Test models. We need an experienced driver," he laughed.

Their conversation ratcheted me to the top of a coaster, the weightlessness before free-fall.

" . . . yeah, bring a box, we can always use them," Don finished up. "Patch can't get hard without them. Just buzz at the gate. Call me afterwards. Bye." Don hung up and addressed us. "Well, he wants you both. That OK, *Jeremy*?"

"Yeah . . . it's just, I didn't know it was gonna be tonight, but . . . You want me to take my shirt off?"

Now comes the good part. Right?

"Oh, if you really *want* to," Don replied, replacing the phone on its cradle with measured ease. His gaze was delicate, momentarily.

Then he yelled at Craig, "Doesn't he have a great chest? Perfect. Leave it off until Chas comes. You can greet him at the gate shirtless, he'll love it. You an athlete?"

"Yeah, I'm at a Main Line school. Soccer." None of this was true, nor was I making it up; it was just . . . coming out.

"Tell you what, Jeremy," snarled Don, animated, hands jumping. "I was eighteen at 'Nova, I put myself through school doing this. 'Course, now I'm the Don. I'm Sicilian (you get it? The *Don!*) but now I'm on the other end. Sure, every now and then for the guys that want me specifically, hell *yes* I'll go over in leather and bring my chains. They get enough of me to last them a long time!" Don's laugh degenerated into a phlegm-choke. He spit into a Kleenex. "We'll try you out," he croaked, "and work from there. What did you say you'd done before?"

"Oh. On my own I accepted some offers from guys at health clubs, for modeling and stuff." I couldn't stop lying. I told myself to quit it. "I'll do it," I said, not confidently, like I wanted it to come out, but strangely resolute. "No problem."

"Are you gay?" asked Don. "You act real straight."

"I think," I started. "I think I like . . . I think I like guys more?" I couldn't tell whether my answer was another question. My mom's running joke was that Midwesterners needed two question marks to identify what the real questions were. As in, *I went to the Queen concert? Last weekend? And do you know who I saw there?? Golda Meir!*

"When was the last time you were with a guy?" asked Don, jerking me out of the fantasyland of dead Freddie Mercury and into the static electricity of now. I could feel the hair on my neck stretch away, seeking contact, recalling Cal.

Fourth grade. Blond hair blue eyes buck teeth soft lips. Back when I only wanted to be Ivan. Why'd he have to say that? Cal's piping soprano, as clear as the recorder he used to play. *Be Jenny. Otherwise* . . . Quick, one more lie:

"I was with a guy this summer." It could have been true. It didn't matter anyway, I thought.

"Well, Charlie likes spontaneous incest, that's what turns him on. You guys work it out. He's been with me for years. Comes down from Camden, twenty-five minutes away. That gives me fifteen to talk and ten to clean up the mess. You guys are going to do it down here in the living room. When you start doing incalls here, you can also use the upstairs bedroom, which is Craig's room right now. That's where him and me are gonna be.

"Okay, we gotta get a few things straight," Don continued, his intensity commanding our attention. "Never work on your own or with any other agency. It's way too risky. You kids stick with me. We're really close around here. I have parties every couple of weeks or so, everybody comes and hangs out. This ain't as easy as you think. There are some trolls who come in here, way I feel is, as long as they're paying, you're staying. Once in awhile, you're gonna get someone who might not turn you on. So you better get used to using what you got to use."

I squirmed on my love seat, in over my head. After Aleksandr, I told myself, I deserve to be punished. This whole time I'd been think-ing: dinner, a movie, then maybe a handjob or something. Wasn't that what an escort was? I stole a look at Ashley: was he cute, was he scared? No on both counts. The only gay sex I'd ever seen was last week, in the steam room. They made it look easy. Trying to seem self-contained, I watched Don's arms lock together as he breezed through entrapment.

"Don't you ever admit this is about sex. That's how Sydney Biddle Barrows got caught. One of her girls panicked. Turned in the greatest madam of them all." He whistled through his teeth at this stupidity and rushed on. "What else? Well. I'm always careful about dangerous clients. We don't do that shit they do other places, no blood play, no piercing, we don't get drugs for nobody unless they want poppers or coke, then you tell them to get in touch with me personally. I have about 50 percent repeat customers here, and we know how to handle them," he barked.

Ashley rubbed a thumb and two fingers together. "What about the money?" he grinned.

"Did I tell you I paid my way through 'Nova doing this?" Don bared his yellow lower teeth in a smile. "You shoulda seen me," he rose, moving my way. "Wiry little guy with an eight-inch rod the men loved." He helped me off the couch. "Let me show you boys a picture." He walked to a closet in the far corner of the living room. "I keep this in my memento shoebox here. Check it out, I'm ready to go." Don handed me the picture. "Baby I could go all day!"

The picture was worn smooth on the edges, a wallet-size black-and-white. A boy reclined on a cot, hands near his jutting cock. He wore a gratified smile and looked straight at me. Stimulated by an unknown nostalgia, by the boy's tumescence, I thought of my long-held desire to be frozen in motion, forever admired. Then I faced today's Don and saw the specter that the photo really was. His skin was leathery; his face bristled. Even his eyes had changed, suspicion narrowing them over time to black, sunken points. Naked, I guessed, he would be a tragedy. I couldn't stand knowing how powerless I was to free the boy in this scrapbook photo from his eventual result. It was only going to get worse. I covered his dick with my thumb.

"I still see you in that," I said, another lie, and handed the picture to Ashley. Spooked, he took a quick look, laughed nervously, and handed it back to Don.

"I don't think I've changed that much. Little older, sure. What can you do, enjoy it while you got it. Make it work for you. And here's how the money works," he said, replacing the shoebox and grabbing fresh linens. "You make thirty-five bucks each for this one, because you're sharing him. Normally it's seventy an hour. More than an hour, or long trips, those are both negotiable. He leaves the money on the dresser, so don't you take money from his hands or even pick it up until he's gone. That's how you get busted. You give the money to me, and I cut you your share. You guys ready? Come on. You can help me make the bed."

We moved the chairs in front of Don's memory lane and converted a couch. White towels fell from the sky. Ashley and I avoided each other's eyes. The buzzer rang. Don trampled upstairs, shouting instructions about the gate and the time.

"Whatever you do, Jeremy, keep your watch on!" he said, and disappeared.

"How are we supposed to forget he and Craig are right upstairs?" I asked out loud.

"Who cares?" asked Ashley, sarcastically. "Gonna get the door?"

I made sure my rope was fastened and meandered the front path, groped for the gate in the warm rain that had started to pelt fiercely. "Hello," I said to a sandy-haired man in a dark business suit. "My name is Jeremy." I led him backward to shelter, so he could stare at my chest, and checked my watch. 9:15.

"Ashley, this is . . . Chas," I said to the thin kid standing uncertainly by crisply tucked sheets. "Chas, Ashley. Where d'ya live, Chas?"

"Jersey. You boys on the clock?" We nodded. "Then let's skip the small talk, we all know those aren't your real names anyway. You're brothers, right?"

"No!" I started. "We just met—"

"—We're cousins," Ashley interrupted. "First cousins."

"Why, that's fine. Decided to come over after school?"

"Yes," Ashley said. "I've wanted to for awhile, but he—" he glared at me "—needed to be convinced."

"Swell. Well boy howdy, Jeremy, since you're the shy one, I'd like to see you take off your older cousin's shirt and pants."

Ashley half-smiled, his shirt almost totally unbuttoned.

"Stop what you're doing, Ashley. Let your cousin do it."

Ashley stuck out his tongue. I sauntered over to the kid like I knew what to do, like I liked his looks. He leveled a disturbing glance, at once flirty and scornful, a hand on his hip, as if to suggest I wouldn't have had a chance with him if we weren't getting paid. Or if we weren't *cousins*. I could not stop this. What I could do was unzip Ashley's black jeans and tug them down his body, taking care not to touch his skin, not if I didn't have to.

My eyes were at the level of Ashley's lavender bikini briefs. They made him look like a lead in a porno version of *Lord of the Flies*. Lord of the Fleas? I stepped aside so Chas could admire this child.

"That's very nice," said the man coldly. "Take off his panties and suck his dick."

Just like that, still in his suit. My eyes conveyed an apology to Ashley. He sneered back at me: *what's your problem, get on with it already*. I slipped the boy's soft underwear off, glanced down. The gray hue was starting to purple. I'd never given anyone a blowjob before. I kneeled on the thin brown all-around and felt the concrete in my knees. When I was a kid I wished we had that stuff, so I could pretend it was Astroturf when I played indoor football. Proving something, I massaged Ashley in my palm, felt him start to stiffen, and looked into his eyes. Ash stared off to the kitchen, or the front door, disembodied.

Rolling his cock over, I took the tip in my lips. It tasted human, like any flesh, the area around it more pungent, its faint reminder of urinals. Could you get anything through oral sex? Would Ashley tap me before he came like Cal did with his first girlfriend, Debra? (Laverne, who not coincidentally had been Debra's best friend, told me this one day during a particularly thrilling matinee involving young men, skinny-dipping, and pianos.) Ashley grew inside my throat until I couldn't move him around without choking, so I pulled off after two gags and suggested we go on to something else. I was sure that if I kept going I'd puke all over his chest.

"Okay, why don't you take off your clothes?" said Chas, observing.

"Sure." I let my jeans down in one stroke and rolled them, with my shoes and socks, under the convertible bed. Naked, approaching. What should I do now? I feathered my fingers through the man's pale, thinning hair. The stalks he'd gelled across his forehead felt like sticks of hay. I leaned in for a kiss.

"What the fuck are you doing?" he asked, batting away my arm at the elbow. "Stop! Jesus. Anybody want poppers?"

"Yes," Ashley announced. Prefigured by his thick erection, absurd against his frail body, he swung across the room and took a vial from Chas's pocket, cracked it open, inhaled deeply. Chas opened another and undressed. There were specific faces my fantasies projected, and they didn't belong to these perfectly average, horny guys romping around with pill containers. They tried to get me hard, don't get me wrong, but in the end, with an eye on the clock, they had to give up. Closing my lids, I imagined myself back in the sauna, a temporary sacrifice. I couldn't watch them work themselves over me. I only sensed their heat dripping, sticking to my skin like melted wax, gluing me to the convertible couch and I shut my eyes tighter, out of my mind, burning when someone roughly wiped my chest and stomach. There was peace in their decelerating breath, the Frankincense sweetness of amyl canisters, the rebound of the springs when they rolled off the pullout.

Once Chas was dressed, I got up, held my jeans by the waist. Ashley made sure Chas did his drop on the dresser, then counted the cash. I led our first client back to the gate. It had started to pour.

"Thanks for being so understanding," I said to old Chas. He unleashed his umbrella and stepped underneath, holding it away from me. Since I couldn't look him in the eye, I glared into the gale. "It was my first time doing this, I was nervous, it wasn't you. I'm sorry."

"Don't worry about it, kid. See you later." He vanished into puddled streets like arsenic swirled into black tea.

Back inside, we silently yanked the sheets off the pullout and folded it back into shape. Don came downstairs, exchanged our money, and exhorted me to stay and talk and do another one.

"I need to eat," I said. "I'll call you tomorrow or the next day."

"No. *I'll* get in touch with *you*."

Ashley, still nude, lounged on the transformed couch.

I gathered my shirt, shoes and socks and talked real fast. "Remember I don't have a phone yet, don't know when I will but I'll call real soon, I'm sure, so thanks and nice meeting you all, OK?"

Craig reappeared to escort me to the gate.

"How was it?" he asked, in the downpour.

"I don't know," I yelled over the rain. "I didn't know what to do."

"You get used to it, like anything else. Ever go to any bars? You never know, you might find . . . Go to Woody's." Craig pressed the button, let me out.

"What do you do about AIDS?" I shouted from the other side of the iron, which turned out to be harder than I thought to bring up because nobody had mentioned it yet.

Craig looked embarrassed, maybe for me. "They say you should use condoms if there's *fucking*. Don don't give a shit, he'd probably want it to be unsafe, his clients sure do." The brief maelstrom was petering out, and he lowered his voice. "You don't have to let them pressure you. So use a condom if you want. Next time you're down here I'll give you some, but you should probably have them around anyway."

I thanked him, fished out a smoke, and backed off, lingering in the drizzle, ashamed and defiant about carrying this out. Underneath, this black hole of fear. I bought a cheese steak at WaWa, strode back up South, set my alarm for registration. I went to the sink to wash my hands, flexed in the mirror, stripped off my clothes again.

My lips seemed different, swollen. Could people tell you sucked cock from looking at your mouth? Kleenex scraps had bonded to the dried semen in my navel. I flashed back to my mental picture of Craig's living room, distantly picturing my body in the middle of the action. I took myself to orgasm and the images left me desolate, like a cinema after the credits have rolled and the house lights are on and they're prying the candy from the floor.

Movie theaters are portals to space travel. You go into a matinee and you don't change but when you leave the day is gone, the world has moved on. I didn't think time was real. Moments lay piled on top of each other like cards. As soon as you look twice the deck's already reshuffled. All the order has just broken down.

Now, rinse, and look at that, all clean.

100 Ways to Kill Yourself

The Germans and I are trying to solve the puzzle of time. Dad has written me a postcard. On the front's a big blond girl in braids and a blue dress holding out a coiled knockwurst on a silver platter. *Imagine time as this knockwurst. It looks smooth from far away but when you get very close the lining's uneven. Under a microscope, you see that the surface is incongruent and ragged, with no discernable pattern, like hard-ridged salami. I'm eating fresh walnuts from my friends' backyard. Back to WI in Jan.* I wish he would hurry.

School has started, ushered in by the meter-maid ticker-tape parade on my windshield. Every morning I clear their leftover confetti and throw it away. I'm taking a photography class, one multimedia course, and something in film about Marlene Dietrich. The best street queens can walk like her. Bergman's camera loves her hands. *Hands are our spokesmen,* the handout reads. *Hands are our slaves.* In my hand is my old high school folder, my panicky afterthought: did

I hide it well enough this time? Is the terror once inspired by my ex-cised medical pictures indelibly attached to my desire? I am afraid of this, if I'm no longer afraid of being found with the images. I own these boys now. I possess them and they possess me and I repossess myself. I guess I could still be arrested for possession, but I've found something new to scare me, anyway.

This will become a darkroom ritual, unfolding stolen boys, matching them to their negatives, the reproductions I've taken in the lengthening sun shafts on my sloping carpet. Mummification has left them ravaged and frayed, creasing into new cuts as cold knuckles clenching. Their weathering is the incongruence of time: genitals and torsos intact, necks nearly severed by wrinkles, barred faces still smooth as peach fuzz. (The Stolz boys are the exception, but I have other plans for them.) I wash my hands before I touch the shiny skin containing their dimensions. I superimpose them against each other on the enlarger surface, wait for their chemistry to emerge. Would "CJ (19)" and "JJ (15)," those slow-maturing Califor-nia boys, like to stand on a park bench in Rittenhouse Square with "Hypogonadal Boy," wearing acorn codpieces and black eyebars, Marlene Dietrich posing salaciously nearby? Or would they be bet-ter off alone, separated, fading like ghosts into a forgotten sandlot's dugouts, genitals removed via chemical burn?

I can't tell. They all look good to me. They're really photogenic. They really shouldn't be so exposed. Hands are my censors, and I photocopy mine in fists and birds, open palms and middle fingers, pimp-slaps and peace symbols and guns. I sink my fingertips into a sponge of red stamp ink, leave my prints all over their bodies.

Outside, the whores are out to play. They like certain hours: 8 a.m., 5 p.m., 2 a.m. Lombard's a residential one-way heading out of the city to the Baltimore Pike, and commuters use it to bypass busy Chestnut and Walnut until the freeway ramps at 26th. Still, it's only two lanes and the slow lights and inexorable backups ensure that hookers can do walk-ups. I watch them from under the scaffolding.

Certain cars circle over and over, and those are the ones the young girls stroll up to.

I don't know what to do about Don. I tell myself I should at least call him to see if he'll let me reproduce his old porn pic.

He gets right to the point. "Wanna to do another appointment? Incall only. Where do you live?"

"Around 16th and South, why?"

"So I can send Buster over. He's real quick, ten minutes and you're done. Sixty bucks. He'll give ya eighty, gimme the change. And I got you an overnight Saturday in Jersey. Two-twenty plus train fare. Likes those real young boys. Pretend you're fifteen."

"How's Ashley doing?" I bite my lower lip to calm down. Across the street, the leaves on the top of a wire-girded oak sapling gleam an early magenta, glossed lips in the midday fall sun.

"What do you care about him?"

"I don't know, he seemed real into it, maybe he wants the overnight."

"Ashley gets enough business. Just because he can take two dicks at once doesn't mean he can be at two places at the same time." Don's laugh was a forced, malignant staccato. "You want to do this or not? You want the money? You got two seconds, he's on the other line."

"Okay." I don't even think it has anything to do with money.

"What's your address?"

"1536 Lombard. 3F."

"Great. Hold the line." Don clicks off. "OK Jeremy, you go on down without a shirt on, meet him at the door when he buzzes."

"Yeah, I have to. I mean, we can't buzz from our apartments. I'm nervous about my neighbors, you know, what will they think?"

"How are they gonna know? You gotta announce your visitors?"

"No, but—"

"Tell him you're house-sitting, it's your friend's place. Fifteen minutes. You better get ready. Drop the twenty by eight. Bye."

I barely have time to hide all my photos and some personal stuff before Buster buzzes. I just stuff what I can grab into my closet. On my run downstairs I shrug off my T-shirt and tuck it in the back of my pants. I fling the front door open to a sidelined linebacker on a 'roid rage, wedged into a three-piece suit.

"Don call you?" he asks, militant.

"Huh?" I stall. I think I might just close up shop.

"Don't give me this bullshit," he says, and pins the door open with his left shoulder.

I buckle. "Oh yeah, I'm Iva—Eye—I mean, Jeremy." My real name just sounded dumb, like a stutter.

"Don't need to know your freaking name. You showing me up-stairs or do I find it myself?" He moves in fast and I backpedal up. By the time we get to three, our last push to the summit, he's bent over, hands on his knees, breathing hard. His tie looks too tight. His face is mottled, contorted, on the verge of explosion. I can just go in there and lock the door and never come out ever . . .

"This isn't my place. I'm just house-sitting for a friend," I say fast and loud, immediately doubtful that either Buster or the neighbors believe this. I whisper, "He's getting home real soon so I don't think this is gonna work."

"Sure," snorts Buster, rising up. He points to his watch. "Better get cracking, you're on the clock, right?" He stares, hard and emotionless. I'm searching for something in his face, but it isn't there and I don't know what I'm looking for anyway. "So where the fuck we doing this," he asks, "the floor?"

My legs are shaking so hard my foot's tapping the floor. I clench them to a tremble. "Whenever the bills hit that mantle, we can head up to the loft." I try to be steady but I'm worried I quavered.

He grunts in response, his eyes the slash between twin blades, but he reaches into his pocket and peels off paper from a billfold. Show-ing off, I muscle up the loft's overhang while he tries the ladder. I've never heard wood cringe like that. It reminds me of the screaming when someone in the cannery lost an arm. We reconvene over the white wooden slats on my boyhood twin mattress.

"Do you want me to take my pants off?"

No one likes a beggar and, besides, Buster's face muffles my words with the heat of just-used sandpaper, with the afterburn of a frozen wart. The colder you get the more numb you are. When men die of exposure at eight thousand meters they're sometimes so numb that it's pleasant. They strip off their parkas and bask under cover of stars. Up there, in my glacier, I might not feel him masticating my neck, stuffing his penis in between my teeth. I might not hear him say, *You like it, don't you, when-I-fuck-your-mouth, cocksucker,* when I'm too still to nod.

Doomed mountaineers have moments of clarity before death, short breaks from blossoming delusion caused by hypoxia. This wouldn't be so uncomfortable if I didn't suck at giving head so much. He grabs my head by the curls and forces himself in. I gag every third thrust, then every other, then each. *Lick my balls and keep my meat inside.* The joints under my ears pop like bolts on beams. I suckle his testicles like they're neglected runts until he pulls out and sprays his mucilage on my eyelids. I hear the faint zip of his fly, the grunt as he tightens his tie. I wipe my eyes. Where my spine presses into drywall he vibrates, earthquake in the doorframe, thunder on the stairs. The storm blows by. The plaster breathes a sigh of relief.

I hang from the loft and let my hands peel slowly off the edge, drop my feet to the floor, back to base. All I can see is his face in sharp focus. My neurons propel him back into my head. Otherwise, I'd get stuck seeing him come back to me in unbearable clarity, without blurring and fading, without him ever really leaving. And so I replay the scene over and over until I sense him as vague spirit, bearing just the remnants of its form.

So I can say, this *happened;* and, it's not really so bad after all.

A shaft pokes between clouds and onto my industrial carpet. We're millions of miles away from where the sun cast those beams, but the rays have taken just eight seconds to arrive, always at the speed of light, bending space and time and all those dimensions too small to see or measure. On their way they've passed meteorites, cosmic dust, gaseous detritus, atmospheric shields. Photons never die.

They just keep bouncing around forever. The history of the universe is in my room.

In an hour or two, I am no longer considering Buster, but I can't stop thinking about ways to kill myself. The easy ways: revolver cooling a forehead, a guillotine's gravitational drift, or a leap out the window. The slow ways: cigarettes, sex, exposure. The pretty ways: a shiny black gun in a slick pink ass. A slim syringe anchored in a plump penile vein, red handkerchief winched around the scrotum, a tourniquet. A noose looping over a swanlike neck. A razor blade sinking into a wrist. Deep-throating an exhaust pipe. Out in the rain, face and shoulders corroding in pale petals. Emerging from a mine, streaked with soot like war paint. Surfacing from a river, covered in sewage and slime. Blood trickling from nose and mouth, globe resting against my face. The world will kill you and I want to do it a hundred ways. Mr. Yuk always said for the suicide prevention speech that there were warning signs. For every successful suicide, there were eight to twenty-five previous attempts. I'm sure I can do better than that.

The prop room in the school theater has almost everything I need for now. Another honors system steal, but they'll get it back tomorrow. Back again at home I remove my clothes, set the tripod and timer, and get to work. With three guns and two principal orifices, plus symbolic favorites like daggers and arrows and nipples and eardrums, I'm well on my way.

It's almost dark by the time I'm done. I grab a jacket, the cash, and my Pentax and flash, head out the fire escape and into the crack lot. Hucksters are killing the twilight.

My friend my friend you want some smoke?

Hey young pup you looking for a bitch to call your own? Whassamatter doncha swing that way you like sniffing assholes?

Hey lost boy white boy whitey come here come here I'm not gonna hurt you show some respect come here rude boy rude boy!

Here baby you're looking for pussy check me out sweet thang don't listen to them!

The polite thing to do is wave, say hey, but that invites intimate talks about my cash on hand, so I make lame gestures and veer around corners. By the time I get to Don's I'm winded—too many smokes—and rest against the gate. It unlocks suddenly and I crumple not so gracefully to the sidewalk. Don's inside with a coiled, compact man wearing a dark beard and black denim. He looks like he should have an eye patch.

"Jeremy, hello. This is Sonny the porn star."

"Yeah," says Sonny, laconically waving over. It's a move to practice.

"Hey," I return the dismissive wave. "Here's your twenty, Don."

Don yanks it from my hand like Rittenhouse pigeons snatch sandwiches. One early morning taking pictures in the square, I watched two pigeons fighting over some crack that someone must have jettisoned, and that the cops hadn't found, but I overexposed the negatives and lost the roll.

"You want to get into porn, Sonny here is the man to talk to, isn't that right Sonny boy?" He takes a *billet-doux* out of his back pocket, unclasps, counts his money, and replaces the works. Sonny's eyes never leave the roll, but he manages a shrug.

I unveil the camera from my jacket. "Actually I kind of want to talk to you about taking a picture of your picture."

Don smiles thinly. "How much?" he asks.

"Excuse me?"

"How much will you pay me for the privilege?" Don's smile widens.

"You want me to pay you? It's for a project."

Sonny's eyes glaze over. He stretches a leg along the couch, reclines, and lights a Marlboro.

"You want to look at me forever," Don snorts. "You're probably selling it to a magazine."

I wonder how exactly I'd accomplish that. When was this taken, 1958? "No problem. You get 50 percent from any sales I make."

"Give it to me in writing, and I'll think about it. I still need you for the Mayor on Saturday."

"Yeah."

"The Mayor should treat him good, don't you think?" From behind the couch, Don jabs Sonny's leather jacket with a long finger.

"That old fuck's still around?" Sonny asks. "Well, shit." He looks me over, cracks a grin. "He'll treat you real nice," he says, and they both laugh.

"He likes to drink," Don says, in the way of a briefing. "Call me tomorrow."

"Right."

It's time to get lost. I find a diner in the middle of town and order a three-egg omelet. It comes on a bagel. Philly food makes me think I'm Rocky, ready to run up the stairs at the Museum of Art. American cheese sizzles against the roof of my mouth.

On 16th and Mole, a woman offers me another blowjob. *Ten bucks baby just ten bucks.* I demur. But, on second thought . . .

"Do you know where I can get some dope?"

She nods, says, "Wait here," clicks around the corner, and brings back a man in a Phillies cap. She doesn't need to point me out, and when her man comes to me, she dodges into someone's passenger seat and disappears.

"What you want?" asks her friend. "What you looking for?"

"Just marijuana."

"Oh, you want some weed?"

"Yeah, maybe two dime bags." I'm not nervous anymore.

"Okay. Give me the bills, I'll be right back."

"Naw. I'll pay when you bring it, or come with you."

"What you thinking, you can't come with me! You'll get shot, little whiteboy. Listen I'm trying to help you out. But we can't just stand here talking. Berries might think something's going down."

"It's not happening, then." I look around, don't see any cops. I don't think they dare patrol too far beyond South. In Milwaukee the cops never enter black neighborhoods.

"Tell you what," says the dealer, adjusting his cap. "My girl said you wanted *dope*. But you want weed. I *got* dope." He fishes out a green box of Newports. "You hold this while I score you some weed," he says. "That way you know you can trust me."

"What would I want your squares for?"

The man gets closer, opens the box. "That's crack." He indicates three vials inside the case. "I sell crack. That's my product. You give me the twenty, hold on to this, I'll be back with your dime bags."

Totally confused, I go along with this.

He vanishes.

I grip the Newport box and wait. Forms move through the ruins of buildings. Wind ducks and intensifies through huge holes in the walls, sending up cigarette butts, dirt, shoelaces, and window glass in the city's version of tumbleweeds and tornadoes. In twenty-five minutes, pissed but too scared to race through the galleries, I wander back to Lombard. My metal pipe's in my closet. The Newport box is a crack house all its own: tattered cardboard sides holding three plastic cylinders. I take one out and unscrew the red cap, let the cold white pebbles fall into a palm like hailstones. Do they really change your body's chemistry so you forget everyone who ever loved you? I'm not sure it'll work but I can see myself trying.

I put the rocks in Mom's cookie tin and drop down the fire escape to the Broad Street library. I slide down the stairs to the basement, pulse fleet, to find the early works of Baron Wilhelm von Gloeden, the German expatriate who made a career at the turn of the century photographing young Sicilians. Sadly, I'm finally getting bored with the faceless forms in my closet. They're slightly *too* impassive. I'm elated to see the baron's subjects still sharing so much with the world, specifically me, a hundred years after he captured them at such physically formative stages. I've wished I could be like them, in some fashion, ever since I first jacked off in the mirror.

These pictures are direct. In dull solid grays, no sepia here, the models look bored, musty, archival, as if waiting a century for me to make contact. Their quality would be better on the glossy stock of 1950s medical textbooks. Instead they're like the 1932 *Journal of Nervous and Mental Disorders:* Their luster is muted in archaic technique, in the flesh of old boys now dead or using walkers. They're mute. "Hey there," I whisper to a kid clambering up a pillar. "How's it hanging?" I just wish he could hear me.

They're wary. Nobody smiles. The older boys are somber, aware but resigned. They either stare at their penises, musing on their new status as sex objects, or glare at me, saying *Hey, let's get this over with.*

Hearing footsteps on the stairs, I feel past my hard-on for some pocket change, scamper to the Xerox. The first boy I run off is a kid who looks, by current standards, to be about thirteen. Maybe he was sixteen in 1898 when the baron immortalized his profile. Wearing a sailor's cap that tilts off the back of his head, the curly-haired kid stands, facing right, against a dark Indian tapestry. His nose hooks through a paisley. His arms are thin, like a girl's; his breasts are tiny sacs, his musculature an underdeveloped afterthought. His ribs are caged translucently beneath the skin, interrupted by a vaguely protruding stomach. His right hip's thrown back, amplifying his ass. He has no hair on his torso, and it doesn't look like there will be any, for quite a while, *forever . . . really.* Black curls start just before the base of his penis, drifting above, controlled. His penis slithers across the page, just about to swell, mocked from above by a bulbous calla lily that he holds erect. His cock strains away from his hip, foreskin stretched up to his glans. I focus a second more, spin a quarter into the machinery, and press the green button. Mine forever.

A student passes me hurriedly.

Rather than make eye contact, I shuffle over to cover the duplicate. The kid disappears into the stacks. I fold the boy into my back pocket, and name him: Sal, for salacious and *salir,* to go.

Next image: another youth, around the same age as the first, standing against a similar tapestry. He has a face like a bird, an aquiline nose, small pale eyes you have to squint to see. His chin is tilted skyward. The overcast tones conjure either a cavernous room or the eerie darkening of thick, threatening clouds. His lips purse in apparent dissatisfaction, impatient with the baron's tedious exposures, or discomfort.

He's further away from the camera than Sal, standing between two pillars on some scaffolding, probably; but the way it's cropped makes it seem like the boy's a centerpiece on a mantle, living ivory, a little statue, another of the Gloeden's props. Everything about him is smooth as enamel; even his legs, imperfect and crooked, as if a result of the baron one day deciding to fuck around with clay. The light clipped hair on the top if his head is the only thing giving the boy away as alive, but he's probably not anymore.

Wishing that the boy *(Paolo?)* was closer to the camera, I solve the problem by giving him 110 percent. I heighten the contrast to lighten his body and darken his developing hair. I pocket Paolo, hear books moving around, and flip through the group scenes for a final portrait.

Romeo's different. Probably seventeen, his model face, sinewy arms, and sitting position separates him from Sal and Paolo. He has dense, curly black hair on his head and above and along his penis, which poses thickly on a bench covered by dark cloth. Romeo's in a zone, lost in thought, surveying himself, stretching, blooming, beautiful. Is it contemplation, desire, or is he just willing himself not to harden? What does he think about the small white Ganymede figurine standing beside him?

I turn Romeo over the glass, slam the lightproof cover on him, imagining I'm rendering the colorful scene two-dimensional, as the baron. Like life, but lifeless. That serial killer from my hometown tried to put his boys into comas so he could have them with him always, so they wouldn't just leave after an hour, but it was harder to do than he thought. I clone Romeo just as presented, before I'm driven to kiss the book or come in my pants. I quarter the last keepsake, stuff it behind my left buttock, and avoid the searching student, who stares in consternation at the rack. By pretending he isn't there, I almost knock him over when I slip the baron's subjects into their original position, as if they'd never been touched, as if I'd never been there at all.

The Mayor of Nowhere

Under the sheet, my timed flashes were a lightning storm. I was mimicking the inside of a photocopier. I hadn't counted on my phone ringing, and I dug myself out of my igloo and groped for the vibrating lump.

"Hey, this is Eye." I wanted it to be Dad.

"Jeremy," said Don. "What the fuck are you still doing here?"

"How did you get my number?"

"Caller ID. In this business you need all the help you can get. Why the *hell* haven't you called me today? Why aren't you on the train I told to you take? The Mayor's going to be very angry."

"You didn't tell me any specific train. Besides, I thought that was tomorrow."

"His plans changed. You have to do it tonight. Hold on." Don clicked off and on again. "That was him. He wanted you on the 3:30 train, but you can get on the 6:30. Gives you an hour to get ready."

This sounded like bullshit, but I guessed I didn't have any real plans. "I don't even know if I'm going to take—this assignment," I said, trying to be cryptic.

"Who do you think I am? Some teacher you can blow off? You gave me your word. Take it or leave it. But don't think you're gonna work for me again if you skip out." It sounded like he was spitting into the phone. Don paused to exhale. "I know where you live, re-member? You do this one, you want to quit, fine, we're all square. Just don't cross me."

My blood pumped hard in my jaw. I didn't want Don here. I cowered back under the sheets.

"You want me on the 6:30 to Trenton." My voice was faint and querulous, like it was coming from a deep crevasse.

"On the New York train. The Metroliner. It's seventy dollars. He'll pay you back. What are you wearing?"

"A pair of jeans, I don't know, a sweatshirt."

"Wear that pink shirt again. Then he'll have someone to pick out. Bring an overnight bag. He'll be drinking in the station bar when you get on your train, but meet him—this is very important—on the street, outside the Trenton exit. Meet me after your train back, on the south side of the station at eleven in the morning and I'll change his check."

"What does he, you know, what does he like?" I asked softly.

"He likes baseball," Don offered. "Listen, I got another call. Any problems, get in touch with me ASAP. See ya." Don clicked off. The lightning flashed again.

"Fuck."

I untangled the sheets as the timer fired a grand finale. I thought to myself that my camera was a renegade Ganymede, stealing Zeus's thunderbolts, and shut it off. Sleepover: toothbrush, change of clothes, jacket, suitcase. The only one I owned had my mom's ini-tials sewn on the leather handle. It was made of a kind of burlap tex-tile, reinforced with cardboard. It was completely falling apart. I thought I might try to fashion myself as a careless rich kid from some prep school nearby.

Outside it had grown overcast, night closing the satin clouds like a coffin. I drew the blue curtain over my Amtrak window, settled into the molded blue cushion and slept until the rails screamed: Trenton. I followed a sandy-haired boy off the train, crestfallen when he dodged the bathrooms. I escalated and hurried out revolving doors. The wind blew off my Alaska hat and I had to sprint down the street to pin it with my shoe, clutching Mom's tattered suitcase closed; the locks had a way of giving. I scanned the loading zone, a mix of business class and homeless class, tailored blazers and soiled tracksuits. A man with a brown tie and trench coat approached, swaying from side to side. He looked heavy, like an average politician, all in all crappy, more City Council than Mayor.

"Jeremy?" he half-yelled, tentative, lumbering across the drive.

I met him halfway. "Hi. The train left late."

"It's fine, there's a bar across the street." I looked up and wondered how much of his life he spent there, looking out the windows, trying to figure out which boys were his. "C'mon, my car's right over here. Have a nice ride up?"

"Sure. How far is your place from here?"

"About twenty minutes. It's in Cherry Hill."

"Is that close to the Verrazano Bridge?" Mom and I had taken that to visit Joan when we went to New York, when I was thirteen. "Can you show me when we pass it?"

"Yeah, you can see it from the highway in the daytime." He unlocked the passenger door of an American car. "What's your hat say?"

"Oh, it's this bar—it says, Fo'c's'le Bar. Short for forecastle, you know, like on a ship. I used to hang out there when I was in Alaska last summer." I liked the hat for its illusory patch, woven with a Tlingit's profile whose nostril was a naked woman's bush, his big nose her thigh: more than meets the eye.

He drove across a bridge. The supernatural yellow glaze of the coastal sky silhouetted Trenton's distressed skyline. The light was like a subway station, atmospheric rime coated with grime.

"That is such a coincidence," the man went on. I snuck a look at the watery, diluted blue of his eyes. His forehead was gray, his cheeks and nose red and polypy. "One of my favorite guys lived in Alaska for a few years. He was just my favorite boy. He was kinda like you. Where were you?"

"Ketchikan. It's the southernmost island, just west off the coast of British Columbia."

"Maybe you were in Juneau for a while. Then, maybe Homer," he suggested.

I didn't see the bait. I thought it was just small talk detritus and swam around it. "I've never been that far west. Or north."

His lips pursed. His eyes bore down the road.

"You name it, I did it. For three months, I painted, filleted down at the docks, worked construction, went hiking. It was pretty sweet."

He grunted and merged with interstate traffic. I wasn't paying attention to where we were going, though I supposed I should. It was so much easier to just relax. It was going to be a long night and I wanted to conserve energy.

"I met some guys at a youth hostel. We built a little home for ourselves in a sandlot that this cannery owned. The lot was called Tent City. There were about a hundred other shacks there by the end of the summer, but when we moved in there were just a few others. And since we were early, we were the first to get jobs."

"Are you telling me the truth about any of this?"

"Huh? Yeah, what reason would I have to . . . ? Well even though we didn't have to pay to camp out, we had to buy food, and the money I made from odd jobs was barely getting me by. We all went up there for money, so we could work and have something to show for it when the season ended. But there was a strike over the money that canneries paid out, and it delayed the start of the season." I was trying to talk local politics. He didn't respond, but I knew he was thinking something smart.

"Now, the fisheries," I continued nervously, "were completely devaluing the price of their salmon. In the world market the retail price was growing for fresh fish. However, since the canneries were using the fish, tossing it into grinders and choppers, to can it, the value of their own products wasn't increasing. And they weren't willing to give the fishermen a good enough deal, so they were selling their fish to other vendors. People would rather buy *fresh* fish, and now the canneries weren't getting any of it, because the fishermen, a totally independent group, all went on strike. And that cost me a good few hundred dollars. But the little guys made a stand, and won! Although we kind of got screwed in the process."

The Mayor didn't react to my homily. It seemed he'd stopped paying attention. Maybe he didn't like to take the job home with him? We exited at Cherry Hill. A long time ago there might have been cherry trees here, but the only things left were blank streets and dead land in the headlights. We graveled down an empty, unpaved road, and pulled into a parking lot servicing five or six condos. The complex was ramshackle, desolate. The man opened the door above a lopsided set of wooden deck stairs and flicked on a light. There was no noise from the other condos. He motioned me into a modest kitchen. It had a small breakfast nook that reminded me of my dead grandparents' ranch house, the ones on my mother's side. They all died young. Her own mother died when she was six. Now there wasn't anyone left, but I remembered the brownies, always with nuts, the colored pencils.

"Let me take your coat," the Mayor said, hanging it in a closet near a portable stereo. "Don told me you were a bartender, too, Jeremy?"

"Oh, yeah, I worked at a strip bar in Alaska, the Marine, for a couple nights, too. Women strippers, of course," I forced a laugh. "I met a nice girl, but she was a dyke."

"Well, then, I'll have a screwdriver. You help yourself. Everything's in the fridge." He left the room, heaved himself onto a couch. "You can toss me your hat." Uncertainly, I flung him my cap. He snatched it out of the musty air by the red corduroy lip.

There was a bottle of Smirnoff in the fridge, and chardonnay, and two limes, whiskey in the cupboard. "And he drinks Johnny

Walker," I whispered to myself, thinking this might go more smoothly if I tried to make fun of myself. I poured an inch and a half of cold vodka into one glass, clinked ice inside in my Scotch. It was only eight. I whispered orders to myself: "Take your time and get him so drunk and keep him up so late we won't have time to have sex. He can just look and admire and we'll fall asleep and then back on the train." With painful care I removed the plastic orange juice pitcher and filled the Mayor's glass. I brought them out to the living room and briefly bowed to the Mayor, who was fastidiously arranging newspapers on a stone table. The apartment was tiny. This had to be his sex house. There wasn't even a dining room. Of course, there wasn't one in my place either, but he had to be at least fifty and why did they call him the Mayor anyway? Maybe he was really interesting. I held out hope and he grabbed his drink. I couldn't give up yet. Maybe he was stashing some good porn or at least some dope.

I slipped more and more alcohol into the Mayor's drinks and more OJ into mine. I opened my apparently cursed pink oxford one button at a time. I didn't want him to get the wrong idea. I wanted him to look and not touch, but he didn't seem to see. He was holding his liquor better than I was, toying, a fat housecat batting a moth.

"I took a boy to LA one weekend," he said, one way or another, for hours. "Got to do it this way." There was no regret in his voice. "No one can know I'm gay. No one suspects." Around midnight, he asked, "What kind of sports do you like?"

"I'm a pretty big football fan. But mostly I played soccer in school."

"What about baseball, Jeremy? I'm a huge fan of the local high school team. They're just the best kids." He closed his eyes, then looked gently at me. "I love watching you play baseball," he said, so softly, as if far away.

"Oh, yeah, I love baseball."

"You can really play the outfield. You can really run. I love watching your ass when you turn your back and race fly balls." He took off his glasses and rubbed the bridge of nose, looked blissfully up at the cobwebbed ceiling.

"My mom used to play baseball with me when she was alive. It was our special thing. She would stand behind the plate on the Little League diamond and hit fly balls with my Louisville Slugger. I'd stand in left field, way back, just before the grass slipped down the ravine. And I got to be so good I could tell by the sound where the ball was headed, how high and how far. We'd play from when the sun went down until it got too dark to see. I could catch everything she hit. Into the purple sky."

I was talking because he wanted to hear more about me, he wanted to understand. I was crying but you couldn't tell. I smoked and cleared my throat, face turned away from him toward the black balcony windows. And the tears on my cheeks might just have been sweat rolling down from my forehead on a hot summer afternoon. At least it was nice and warm in here and I was down to my T-shirt and boxers and socks.

"It used to be my favorite sport," I continued. "Well, team sport, anyway. My absolute first love was gymnastics. I used to be so good."

"You used to be a gymnast? That's great," he slurred, falling back in his chair. The plan was working. "What did you do?"

"Man, I did everything. Flips, kips, hechts, scissors, handstands, giants. But I quit just before high school. Nobody offered it as a sport for boys, they just had girl teams."

"What event did you like most?"

"I liked the high bar," I smiled, flirting a little. "It was the best. I could just swing, around and around, and it was all gravity and me, and the world upside-down and back in place when I wanted it to be. I could control everything with the swing, just my hand muscles, tensing. That's what I miss, besides the trampoline, of course, which isn't an event. The high bar was my favorite."

"Oh yeah?"

"Yeah . . . You're probably wondering why I'm here, huh, why I'm doing this?" I was wondering that myself, thinking of the past like this, my years as Mom's golden boy. I thought it was all over.

"No not at all!" Like a newborn about to be picked up by a stranger, the man's startle reflex jolted him upright and rigid. "Jeremy—"

Too late. The die was cast. He'd listen. He'd heal me by paying attention.

That's when the Mayor rose fast and put a palm over my mouth. I didn't react at all and he wrestled me to the floor. He lifted me by both armpits, walked me down the hall against the drywall and manhandled me into bed, sat on me. I was too shocked to respond. He stuck his thumbs into two points on my neck. The pressure of his touch made my dick swell, sanguine and warm, as the familiar chill trickled from the spot on my forehead where parents kiss children when they're really, really proud.

The knives carved my eyes. White sheet, foreign bed. My mouth tasted like I'd given a tongue bath to a cat farm. Lost. Must be dreaming still. From this spooning inertia, I remembered a man wobbling down the hallway, hands upraised, a baby giant learning to walk. And, from this still life, a moving memory—the man's laborious crash, like a battering ram, shoulder-first into me and then into the drywall that separated the kitchen from the hallway.

The last still resembled a medical photograph: a tongue, chalky white and covered with large bumps, frozen in time. I wasn't ready to examine this. My hangover was a deranged masseur pressing on my temples. The man breathed in stops and starts beside me. Huge, ragged breaths, and then silence; then sputtering, back to life, dying and being born over and over again. I couldn't look at him and wriggled to the far edge of the queen-size, fell back asleep in hazy orange sunrise falling through the window facing Brooklyn. I dreamt of saving an old woman from drowning as she dropped from her ivory ship into the raging blue ocean. I swam with her on my back to the sunny shore, waterlogged, ignoring the nipping deep under the surface from a baby shark wanting to play. As it intensified, I sensed it as a prodding, then a blunt jamming; and flinching out of dreamland and awake again, I felt the weak sun on my back, as if underwater, the dampness, like seaweed, in my ass, and the undertow of a body leaving the bed. The sink ran, the man cleared his throat, gargled, spat. My eyelids closed to let the sun's red imprint wash over me as I took myself in my hands and waited for him to come back, but his footsteps only receded down the hallway.

I staggered into the bathroom and wiped with toilet paper until dry. There was a dot of blood on the last wad, like an adolescent's shaving nick, or a gutted pimple. My eyes froze in their wild dance and fixed upon a plastic bottle of Scope in the half-open medicine cabinet. I spun the top to the floor and splashed the elixir onto a new tissue, spreading it over where I thought the cut was. What do you call an asshole with really good breath? A politician. I flushed, tiptoed back to the room. A sedate calm passed through me as I lay on the bed and let myself reflect in the mirrored closet doors. I masturbated leisurely to the smell of coffee brewing, hoping the Mayor would catch me, but I guessed it didn't matter if he didn't. The sunlight made my shorn body hair look like fine down. The top of my head was blonde, red, and brown, tousled from sleep. My old high school geometry partner once told me she got gang-banged one weekend after she was passed out. She didn't seem all that angry, just maybe pissed off that she wasn't awake to feel what it was like. But she might have been playing it down. I didn't know how to feel. I didn't feel myself come.

In the kitchen, the Mayor looked defeated and gray. He swirled his mug on an orange place mat, faded, frayed, and specked with crumbs. He handed me an envelope and pretended to read the paper. He dribbled Maker's Mark into his coffee. I tried to see his name through the envelope, but it must have been secured, because all I could make out were blue crisscrossing veins.

"What time is it?" I asked. Talking might bring this back to reality. I was beginning to hallucinate a network of purple spots on his face and arms, where they hadn't been last night.

"Almost 9:30," said the Mayor. "You getting the 10:15 from Trenton?"

"Yeah, I have to be back at 11:00."

"Well, we better go then. It's not that short a ride."

"I'm all ready. Wait. Let me find my stuff." My junk was sprayed across the fuck shack. I still wanted to think of it as that. It was too sad to think he really lived here, that this was his life. "Okay, I'm set, whenever you want." I'd lost a sock.

The Mayor grabbed another piece of toast. He was preppy and casual today. There was a baseball game at his alma mater later that he couldn't stop discussing. He gained confidence behind the wheel and looked at me as I examined my zits in the sickly green tint of the passenger side mirror.

"All right, Jeremy," the Mayor said, easing alongside Trenton station.

I thought he was asking after me, not saying goodbye. "Fine. Very tired and hung over though." I half-hoped he'd give a good report: Don could stand to hear a little praise. But mostly I was upset at myself for not waking up, for not telling him off afterwards, even at breakfast, even now. "So what are you the Mayor of?"

"Nowhere." He laughed for the first time and hit the brakes hard. "That's just what they call me. I forgot to tell you," he started, jolting into the curb. "We passed the Verrazano Bridge. You told me to tell you that last night."

"Yeah. I remember. It's okay." Driving to New York with Mom, the seagulls and yachts and the swirling eddies, back when I wanted to run away. I'd finally run away and now I just wanted to get back home. The clock on the Dodge dashboard read 10:07. He handed me a fifty and told me it was train fare. I tucked the cap on my head, gave my thanks, and ducked into the metal boxcar.

On the train I wrote a letter to Theo Sandfordt about how I wanted to love boys the right way. Should I move to the Netherlands? Did Theo have any suggestions? I scribbled these queries in indecipherably small hieroglyphics on the back of the envelope. Then I stared out the rain-streaked windows at dead leafless trees and thought about Anne Frank, tulips, and legalized hash. Back at 30th Street, I checked my watch in the underground track gully beneath the cavernous station. Don was supposed to meet me in ten minutes, by the doors that faced the art museum. I went up an escalator, scoped my territory, lurked in the aisles of the bookstore for a few minutes, and leafed through a book of Muybridge's human motion photos, naked adolescents frogging each other. The bathrooms were nearby, but the loitering men, glory holes, and missing stall doors just reminded me of what I wanted to escape. I bought a trashy paper and sat down in the pews, listened to the rattling drumroll of the schedule updating itself.

I looked again to the revolving doors. Still no Don. A woman talking to her toddler, an elderly couple looking at the McDonald's, a man in a dull gray jacket and shades. A Members Only tag on his jacket. Him. Don. He looked like a mobster with those thick shades. I drew closer. Don ushered me out the revolving doors to a wet bench facing a tier of the museum. We stood on either side and bellowed over the thunder.

"Jeremy! How was it?"

"It was all right. We—I mean, he—got really drunk." I handed him the envelope and made him give it back after he tore it apart.

"Well, he paid you the full amount," Don yelled, flourishing a pocket-wad like DeNiro introducing an Oscar card. "Couldn't have been that much of a disaster. Although you don't look so hot, I gotta say." He counted out my twenties. "Here's the cash."

"Thanks. Do you live nearby?"

"Fairly near. Nobody knows where I live," Don roared, "exactly."

"As long as you do. I got to go." I split before I had to shake his hand. My own hands were shaking and it wasn't even cold. "I'll call you," I hollered over my shoulder, and was down the block, leaving my paper on the bench, its pages flapping in the breeze.

"Soon!" Don screamed after me. "You left this paper—you want it? Jeremy? Jeremy!"

There was no response from the shuffling kid with the baseball hat and tattered suitcase.

I mean, that's not my fucking name.

Poisoning Young Minds

Change is only for people doing laundry, according to the change machine in the laundromat. It's probably right. I don't even want to sort it out, just throw it all in and hope for the best. Sean's shirt spins with my bad-luck oxford and I go across the street for a new *Au Courant*.

I'm done with Don, I promise myself, and peel the slough from the dryer's lint filter. I turn another clipping over in my hand while I watch my clothes revolve in their fast hot orbit. I must have some change left. Heads I call, tails I don't. It's heads.

"Hello," says a reedy voice on the other end. "Ricky speaking."

"Hi, is this the Hot Jock Cleaning Service? Cuz if it is, I want to work for you."

"Well gosh! Okay. What's your name?"

I'm wondering about that. "I guess it's Ivan."

"Okay, Ivan. I'll give you the directions now because I won't know until I see you. You have a pen? You have a car? You know how to get on Interstate 95, heading north?"

The directions to the suburbs are confusing, but I have confidence in my extensive pizza delivery experience. Eventually, I find the Happy Creek Homes after a dazed succession of shiny new strip malls separated by crumbling trestles. Each lot in the subdivision holds an identical two-story brick mini-Victorian with a shingled parapet and a dollhouse portcullis. I feel like I'm in an Advent calendar. My car whinnies and shrieks around the pedicured complex until it comes to an emerald lawn with a statue of a captain in the front yard and a small goldfish pond, Ricky's landmarks. He must have heard me coming, because he meets me at the door.

"Hey! How you doing, Ivan?" He's the picture of a happy Happy Creek homeowner, blond and mid-thirties . . . only he's dressed top to toe in tight black leather. His blue eyes flit over my face in the afternoon sun. "You can call me Ricky."

He extends a hand, ushers me into the living room and onto the sectional, and hands me an application and clipboard, of all things, while he goes to the kitchen to fetch a beer. Another man leans through the front door and slowly staggers in, tall and very thin, a rake with a cane.

"Honey, I'm home," he sings.

Ricky greets him and sits him down while I emphasize my athletic background; these days, of course, about the only exercise I'm getting is masturbation, but I'm not about to tell them that. In the essay section (What skills will you bring to this job?), I write that I'm a scrappy dog who'll lick those floors clean. Ricky's friend leans over my clipboard, long bony fingers on my shoulder.

"The Institute? You didn't tell me that." He glances at Ricky.

"I didn't know! Paul, meet Ivan. I guess I should tell you, Ivan, based on conversation and appearance, you've got a job with my firm."

"I went to the Institute in 1962," Paul offered. "I was a sculptor. Loved the place. So friendly. How do you like it?"

"I love it," I lie.

"Of course, now I'm a lawyer, don't get a lot of time to work on sculptures anymore. What do you think of Ricky's business? I helped him set it up. He's always wanted to do something like this."

"This is my dream!" Ricky crows. "Now shut up so I can teach Ivan how to clean!"

And so he does, leading me up the spiral staircase and past its plaster bust of a disarmed David with Ricky's face (and penis?). From a broom closet, Ricky removes a bucket of cleaning implements: paper towels, mop, solvents, and, of course, the jockstrap that's the centerpiece of his company. He shows me the right way to scour his shiny sink and bathtub: from the edges to the drain, counterclockwise, in the motion of the whirlpool from the faucet water. I swipe at a miraculously carved cane leaning against a wall with my new feather duster. Ricky tells me to vacuum, then dust, carpeted rooms—*not* the other way around. He shows me his office. In contrast to the rest of the house, it's in severe disarray, a spiderweb of wires connecting to any available port. Papers and magazines are strewn across the floor. In the middle of the heap is a red book about how to survive AIDS. I'm not allowed to touch anything in there, so back down to the kitchen, where I scrub and wax a patch of yellow linoleum for practice. Paul rolls a joint and Ricky and I soon tunnel to the lower level with a Polaroid. He flicks on the overheads and we're in a home gym with mirrors on all four walls and a faux Greek pillar pretending to support the ceiling, like Atlas holding a world orbiting just fine on its own.

"Can I take a few pictures of you in the jock, so when a client comes over to pick his cleaner, he'll know what he's getting?" Ricky asks. "You don't have to, but it might get us more business."

Slowly shimmying out of my jeans, I stare into the mirror like the Sicilian models eyeing the lens, warily scanning the glass to read my own face. I find a perfect combination of lust and fear, curiosity and revulsion, hunger and nausea. But that's just how it's always felt. The emotions aren't new, just more intense. I canvas my flesh to see what men see in my body, blink as he takes the picture, say under my breath:

I show myself to you. This is who I am. Ask your questions. I dare you. Look me in the eye. Turn the camera on me.

Ricky is fiddling with his leather vest and pants.

"This outfit," he whispers, "I bought with Paul's money. Six hundred bucks. He doesn't know that yet. He'll probably never know," he says, suddenly dark and faraway. "What he does know," he adds, quickly brightening, "is that there's a cock ring built right into the leather!"

"I knew that whole thing went together."

"Paul, do you need help getting down here?" Ricky calls up the stairs, impatient.

"I'll manage!" Paul yells down, sounding faintly annoyed.

Kneeling on the beige carpet, I arch my back until my curls brush the shags. "Great pose," Ricky yells. I tense for the flash. Paul shows up in white briefs, carrying a stool and a white towel. He leans over the stool like a walker, breathing hard. They take turns shaking the film card.

"Wow," says Ricky, "did you know you had these cute little butt dimples?"

I blush and pose standing for the last photo. I feel like I look happy.

"All done," Ricky says. "Thanks for being so easygoing." He sits on the floor underneath Paul's stool.

"Now you can answer me," Paul says. "What do you think of Ricky's enterprise?" he asks, patting Ricky's head, as if his boyfriend's a pet. "He's waited his whole life to do something like this. We want to do it before it's too late," he says breezily.

"At first I wasn't so sure," I stumble. "But it sounds good. I like the part about fulfilling fantasies."

"Be careful," Ricky cautions. "Some guys might want to take

advantage of you. So just go in there positive that you're in charge, and be aware. We're about fulfilling fantasies . . . but in a safe way."

"We want to make sure," Paul winces, folding his towel into a pillow and sitting back down, "that this is all perfectly legal."

"Of course, if you do want to have sex with them, that's up to you," Ricky laughs. "But I'm telling everybody that's not in the contract."

"Got it." Inspired, I rip off twenty sit-ups, pretending I'm a gay action hero.

Paul jerks off onto the white triangle under his thighs and asks me if I ever wrestled. I deny this and move to the bench press.

"Just make sure the apartment's clean before you start anything kinky, so I won't get professional complaints and have to do the place over again, for free," Ricky advises, pulling on his cock ring.

"Is that about it?" I asked. "'Cause before I leave, I want to know something."

"Shoot," Ricky says.

"I just did!" Paul announces.

Ricky shakes his head, like Paul's an incorrigible six-year-old who had one too many brownies, and passes me the joint.

"You guys seem so . . . comfortable. How did you meet? How many years ago?"

They look lightly at each other. I sit down with them against the pillar.

"We were at a wedding reception," Ricky starts, "in a dance hall. Upstate New York. We both knew the bride's family, but had never met each other. I was having a great time, seventeen, drinking up a storm. The doctors in the psych ward had let me out maybe six weeks before. They said I was cured—*right.*"

"Really? Why were you in a psych ward?"

"Because I was psycho! Not that I got any better in *there.*" He smiles bitterly. "The guy in the next bed just fucked with me—but at least he let me suck his dick a few times! Anyway, I was smoking an ounce of pot every week, skipping school. That's why I got committed.

"So there I was, champagne was in my throat and love was in the air. It really was." He looks wistful for a moment. "Do I think that way because I was so young?"

Paul shakes his head, says, "I felt it too. It was a nice wedding."

"That's what it seemed like. I'd been to my mom's wedding, years before, and boy was that atmosphere funereal. Everybody hated each other. Now here I was, alone. The band was playing Dixie—the groom came up from Mississippi. Across the ballroom, there was a tall, elegant gentleman," he nudges Paul's elbow, "standing alone. Without him, that event would have been nothing. I was thirty feet away and knew I wanted him bad. He turned his head in my direction, and looked at me like the rest of the crowd was just a distraction."

"What did you think when you saw Ricky?" I look at Paul's skinny naked whimsy. Down here in the gym, they are both boys again. We're all boys again here.

"Oh, I thought he was cute. At first I thought he was Hispanic. His hair was black back then. Too young, of course. I wasn't about to initiate and go to prison. He looked younger than he was, like you do," Paul explains, "and I was all too wary of the perils."

"Well I wasn't going to let *him* slip by," Ricky laughs. "So I walked over, asked him his name. Simple as that, like we had every reason in the world to be having a conversation. We made small talk about the wedding. Then I screwed up my courage and asked him if he wanted to dance."

"That's pretty gutsy," I say, thinking of Ryan.

"Horny as a unicorn, more like! Well he refused, but we swapped our handkerchiefs with phone numbers folded inside. Soon we found out we lived less than an hour away from each other. I moved out of Mom's house within the month, which was either May or June."

"June," Paul clarifies. "She made you wait until you cleaned your room."

"And the rest is history?" I ask them. They actually love each other. Paul raises his eyebrows.

"Want to watch some videos?" Ricky asks, his arm around my side.

"Sure." I pick my clothes up off the floor, thinking this might work out. "You're the first boss I've ever had who hasn't treated me like shit right off the bat."

We turn off the lights and help Paul upstairs. The back wall of their hall closet is stacked floor to ceiling with shiny black boxes. They confer quietly and choose a pair of languid identical twins with dark tangled '70s hair who do so much more to each other than I could ever do to my mirror. From the couch to the bedroom, the TV and tape and draped daylight color them lilac. They love each other so much. You can tell by their peaceful violet eyes. They can't be much more than fifteen. They never have to grow, change, die. They want to know if I'd like to take them home with me. I don't have a VCR, so Paul sticks in another instead. My new career splays ahead of me in the form of Mexican dudes getting poled by blonde surfers. It's the best night of my life.

And later, on my loft, between sleep and dream, she comes to me again, a Matryoshka doll in a birdcage. She twists her torsos away from her waists, hollow bodies spinning like tops. She gets smaller and smaller, younger and younger, until she's only a girl with a bag at her feet. *I am ready for a change,* she says, and the wooden girl makes the bag's knot unravel. *It's so dark and crowded in here.* Where will you go? I ask, under my pillow and sheet. The blond girl topples through the bars of the birdcage and into a sand dune. *I'll guide you there. Just listen to me.* She races to the water and opens the bag and the wind blows its butterflies into a spiral, between the blues of the sky and the sea.

It's hard to believe time and space are one and the same, but they are. There's a paradox that makes this even weirder: the faster you travel compared to a motionless person, the more slowly you experience time. An astronaut, for instance, might return to earth after zooming around at the speed of light for a year only to find that sixty years had gone by. But you don't have to go that fast to notice this. There are smaller variations between clocks at rest and clocks that are moving. My dad told me all this once. He said that if you set your watch synchronously with a friend, and then took the train from Frankfurt to Berlin and then returned and compared times, your watch would be ever so slightly slower. I didn't understand it back then, but now I thought I understood. Take my time in Philly: I had only been here a month, and still all this had happened. It's like I never stopped moving, and time slowed to accommodate. When the passing is slow and peaceful, predictable and routine, time speeds up. It's like a vacation: the first few days to a new place are thrilling, packed with stimuli. They seem to last forever. Yet the last few days go by in seconds.

I had settled into a routine, and October to December went by in a Pentax flash. My schedule was pretty basic. Class (if I didn't sleep through the alarm again). Clear parking tickets from windshield (except on Monday mornings, if I didn't sleep through the alarm again). Develop negatives or prints. Lunch—Sherzade on 17th, or Dahlak on the West side—expensive food from impoverished countries, Iraq and Ethiopia. Change into a jockstrap and clean someone's flat. Take some photos and call it a night, rinse and repeat.

Fred, a middle-aged man from North Philly, showed me the drawings he'd done of the neighborhood boys. He lived alone in a narrow rowhouse. He kept his artwork in the attic, which was a guestroom nicknamed (he smiled slyly) "the deserving youth quarters." He refused to let me dust. He refused to let me touch the curling paper, trace the graphite and lead of his neighbors' bodies, but he let me vacuum the living room. By now I knew when I was just a reminder. Fred asked me if it was okay to follow me around, as if that wasn't the point. I jerked off with him to a book on his coffee table: naked Danish teens frolicking in streams. I don't know, they were hot, I just felt like it.

Jason, a lawyer who lived in a brownstone on 10th Street, took to hiring me Wednesday nights to watch *90210*. There was little point schlepping my pail and mop down the alleys if I wasn't going to use them, and I sure wasn't going to use them on Jason's house, but I brought them anyway. The mop was there for support, like a cane, something to fall back on during awkward moments. He plainly thought I was going to shatter his crystal and muddy up the sink, a disheartening but decidedly plausible prediction. Jason finally admitted he had his place cleaned twice a week by a "professional" service. He just wanted to hang out with a kid in a jockstrap, and I'm sure there were many youths who would've happily suffered repeated bouts of Beverly Hills at fifty bucks a pop, but it just made me depressed. *I am being paid to watch crappy television shows,* I thought. By round four (a rerun already, and it wasn't even December), I begged Jason silently to just pay me for sex and turn off the TV: *I'll do anything! Just change the channel!* "You can take off the jockstrap if you're uncomfortable," he finally suggested, watching me slither down his Naugahyde chaise. "Or sit here on the couch with me." Enough gay urban professional intimacy, I thought. "We're a legal service," I maintained, standing and leaning on my mop.

Running up the stairs from my apartment one day after film class, I heard the phone screech like cormorants. I jammed my knee into the banister and launched into 3-F, crawled to the phone and picked it up. Dial tone. *Son of a bitch,* I thought. *What if it's Don?* I turned on the TV, the Eagles were playing, I'm the quarterback, he fires a strike to his wideout just as he gets hit! Hit the floor! If I was back home and nine I'd be running around the junkyard sculpture in the living room in the personalized jersey Mom bought me. Or playing *This Week in Baseball*! Home runs are when I hit the piano with a Nerf ball. Rimmi Catarcove can steal any base he feels like, Rimmi Catarcove steals home!

The floor went thump-thump-thump from below. The phone rang again.

"Hello," I answered, breathless.

"Hello?" said a stranger.

"Who's this?" I asked, on guard.

Andy was an eye doctor from the Philippines. He lived in the medical student housing on 12th. Ricky had given him my number. He'd just moved into the immaculate, tiny apartment, which was a good thing, because I'd forgotten my bucket for once, maybe thinking subconsciously I was headed for Jason's. He greeted me without a shirt. I apologized for not bringing my junk, and realized finally that the word "cleaning" was superfluous to whatever we provided. Andy leaned in and kissed me. No guy had done that since Cal. It mattered so much to me then.

His neck smelled like blazing refuse. We came together without penetration, just guiding and feeling. In the shower he said I was a boy and a man. I quickly discovered that the less I called back the more Andy would call me. After a while, I'd just let it ring, and then, finally, turn off the ringer. Eventually I told him he couldn't keep paying me, it didn't seem fair, and I gave him my address. Late at night he would come to my door and the hoes would shout up that my boyfriend was waiting outside. Sometimes they were so loud ("We know you're up there, hot stuff!") that my neighbors would punch the ceiling and I'd give in to peer pressure and just let him in. When he left, I'd always wonder why I was making things so hard for him, so hard for me, but then I'd just go on avoiding him. I wanted more time to feel lonely. I was trying to be pure.

Besides, I had homework to do.

As partner to 100 Ways to Kill Yourself, I considered Murder in the Lower 48. I wanted to juxtapose my medical boys onto archival photos of environmental catastrophe, one state at a time. I planned to layer these through triple-exposure: boy, catastrophe, map. So I bought an atlas. It turned out that environmental photos were hard to come by and harder to source. As a substitute, I used graphs of mercury pollution in each state's streams, lakes, and coastlines sent to me by the National Wildlife Federation. Poor things, they were only asking for money. According to them, Pennsylvania's power plants pumped seven thousand pounds of mercury into the air every year. When it fell from the sky, it was concentrated via runoff within bodies of water, where it contaminated everything: trout, walleyes, otters, northern pike. And then it simply moved up the food chain, poisoning our nervous systems. Sixty percent of our streams, claimed the authors, were unsafe to fish.

In silver highlighter, I colored in ocean waves and snaking rivers, glued lakes with leaden glitter. I superimposed heads from my eighth grade yearbook onto the *Journal of Nervous and Mental Disease* boys, planted small shiny gray beads in our eyes, turning censorship into poison. Dr. Herbert Stolz, here a series of Xeroxed cutouts, had a corpse to survey in every state. I'd made him a coroner; you're never too old or too dead to go back to school. He dispassionately measured our mercuric eyes with wooden testicular volume balls. He gestured with his pointer to our gonads and nipples. He set calipers to our penises, thermometers to lips. Pallid and overexposed, Jeremy Morris rested on the banks of Lake Michigan; I drowned in the Schuylkill. Our glassine, vitrified eyes made us look like the leaders of a zombie rebellion. There was something I wanted to show. I just didn't know what it was. When I was through with the poisoned states, I laid a car map of the continental U.S. in a tray on my carpet, broke a cheap thermometer over it, and finished off a roll from my loft, documenting mercury's consolidation into chatoyant spheres. When I was done I tossed it into a garbage bag and threw it off the fire escape. Our back lot had seen worse chemicals. What's a little mercury?

Every night, after midnight, one after another, cars would glide noiselessly around the corner and coast into the lot, stall in the ancient half-alley. The street lamps were shattered, or else headlights would never glare down. Halogen zagged off broken windows, aluminum foil, the reprocessed metals in asphalt's upheaval, making the parking lot into a treasure chest or, when the cops came, a risky disco. All those misshapen and worthless old coins only made for bad roads.

Poisoning Young Minds

A hundred years ago, right here, kids dipped handkerchiefs in gaslights, smothered their faces in kerosene fumes. Boys in kneepants sold gum as a pretext: *hey, chew my lips off.* Now, cornered kids heard the whitewalls revolve, the hubcapped rattle of potholes, as cues to materialize from shadowy alcoves. They'd shake off the quickness of spiders, weaving invisibly between blighted doorframes, and offer themselves. No one ever bought these neglected storefronts. The property wasn't worth the loans they'd inherit. Soon the city would buy them from banks, raze them, and pave it all over with the same shoddy composite. But now street queens owned them, as much as they owned the clothes on their backs or the windshielded gazes of circling men. They were there for rent and not purchase. The only things for sale on this street were the drugs.

I recognized what they did by the look in their eyes, the look from my mirror, these unfamiliar kids with familiar expressions. If they saw the same in me, they were more diplomatic, sweetly waving hello now and then. Close-up they weren't kids anymore. The crows had left tracks on their eyes, smearing mascara and tearing away, the marks only sinking in later. Memory, life's slow-acting venom. Some were abscessed along tributaries, as if hummingbirds tapped them for syrup. Their voices would fade into the darkness of tenement houses and crack whores for mothers, monologue whispers drifting in the breeze between buildings. We all have a story to tell. They'd tell each other, in the space of a hit and a nod. In bed, through the screens, they would lull me to sleep with warnings and gossip and brazen carjackings retold over flames under spoons, in competitive huddles of chapped lips and chipped teeth, smooth skin, wild hands.

In the morning rush, I'd take surveillance portraits from my escape, imagining Lewis Hine's mining pictures as backdrop. They were panning for gold, but it was tough to get rich in the 16th Street lot with the mercury and white rocks.

Cleanings turned into massages, and massages turned back into outcalls. Nothing wrong with Ricky's business, only it was new and

I was lucky if I got two gigs a week. I joined another agency, run by a Portuguese weightlifter named Mishael whose main business was breeding Siamese cats. His two floors were pretty and tranquil, over-looking Rittenhouse Square. He had an extensive selection of clean lingerie in the top bureau drawer and essential oils on the night-stand. I specialized in lunchtime rubdowns, mostly married men. I looked forward to them (generally submissive, they didn't try to ante up the massage). Mishael advised that the sooner I flipped them and twisted them off, the sooner they'd be out of my hair. But I figured they paid for the hour, why not let them talk? I thought they were lonely, but it could have been me. They reminded me of Dad. Joe, a roly-poly bear with a wedding band, was proud of his kids. "I just wish I'd had a boy," he'd say each week. "Got the two best little girls in the world, but sometimes I wish I had a boy. Is that wrong?" he asked me, a substitute son tenderizing him in a G-string. "Confes-sion's going to be tough this week!" he'd giggle when I flipped him, like a mischievous altar boy. "Nothing wrong here," I'd say, clamp-ing his thighs reassuringly. "We're not the thought police." That's what religion is for.

Mishael mentioned one afternoon that he was interviewing a new recruit. His interview process was fairly dull, no match for Don's; he took your name, number, preferences (whether top/bottom, incall/outcall, massage/sex), height, weight, hair color, eye color, age, dick size, all based on self-reports. But he was careful not to let the rent boys meet each other. So in the middle of a particularly boring massage with a silent executive, I begged away for water and walked down to the kitchen in a marvelous green cotton bikini. I did this three times, sneaking glimpses of the cute kid earnestly conferring with Mishael. ("What the fuck," Mishael finally acknowledged. "I don't know, I'm thirsty today," I grinned.) With a resigned inevita-bility, he warily introduced me to Sami, who spelled his name out for me. "S-A-M-I," he said. "It's Syrian." I quickened my pace and corkscrewed the exec to climax, then drove Sami back to Drexel. Neither of us knew what to do, so we talked about school (he was in engineering). I was flummoxed and didn't give him my number. Next time I was at Mishael's, I asked him how Sami was doing. "I didn't hire *him*," he said scornfully. "He's too small to be a top and he doesn't want to be a bottom." I wondered about massages but let it go, asked for Sami's number. "I threw it away," Mishael said with finality, and broke up a catfight.

Jeremy turned into Mitch, and Mitch turned into Eye, and I turned into myself. On one date I turned into Kevin-My-Friend-from-Work when a young customer's sugar daddy got home mid-69. The poor disheveled boy raced down the stairs to greet his man while I got dressed and pocketed his ball of hash. The whole thing was my fault; I was late getting there. "See you at the office!" I shouted as I ran out the door—not fooling anyone, but I didn't want to stick around for the payback. I didn't feel guilty at all. He'd seemed like he needed the action. Besides, that's why you get the money first.

In Atlantic City, a Vietnam vet turned the tables on me and gave me a backrub. Across from the Liberty Bell, a very relaxed man took all my junk in his mouth at once, but I didn't get hard. All that work for nothing. Everything else was as much palaver as their hotel rooms, as anonymous and expressionless as jerking off under a tableful of oblivious docs.

We've driven across one-third of the Irish coastline, Dad wrote, *along 2-way roads often the width of one car. You have to wait at driveways or wide spots when another car approaches, and even on wider stretches, each car dodges into the brush on the left of the road to get by. Tiny green fields enclosed by walls of piled stone cover the country. The size of the fields might be the distance their owners were willing to carry the stones to clear them. Sheep graze everywhere. Welsh friends think they've observed lava flows on Mercury! Eating lots of salmon. Off to India, then back to the woods.*

In the same serendipitous mail batch came a forwarded check from Farwest Fisheries, a $1,300 duplicate of one I'd already cashed. I turned the pages in my atlas to find something beyond the lower 48, looking into Mexico. The back of my neck prickled and my face started to burn. I felt strangely like a shell, a capsule, and shut my eyes as my fingers moved down the page. When I opened them again, I was pointing to Playa Azul, between Acapulco and Puerto Vallarta. I bet between the money I was making and this payroll mistake I'd be able to get down there and back over winter break. If I came back at all. Down the middle, then into six sections, I folded the environmental love maps I'd photographed, so they'd look like forgotten old legends.

In December, I worked feverishly, framing these pictures in riverside driftwood and mounting them on my apartment walls. For a final project, an installation piece, I enlarged my three favorite Stolz boys to life-size proportions, shading them in concentric circles: darker on the outside, lightest in the center. I dipped my fingertips in ink and left my mark on their toes, thighs, chests, and lips. I mounted the three youths on layers of cardboard, nailing their navels to three crude platforms I'd mocked up from two-by-fours on extended grift from the shop room. I bought a cheap bow and arrows from a camping/hunting store (fun for the tykes, sharp enough to pierce paper) and a bucket of red Dutch Boy. I put the three targets side by side over a long drop cloth and dipped my arrows in crimson. Then I shot them, coolly, one at a time.

Well, not really. It took a while; I was a terrible shot and kept having to wash down the walls. Maybe I hadn't taken the carpet's acclivity into account. I eventually caught the first boy in the side, the second in the heart, and the last kid right in the nuts. Bull's-eye. The paint was too viscose for splatter patterns, but you don't need an Uzi to kill Saint Sebastian. On the last day of school, I gave a key to each of my professors, and told them my semester's work was in my room.

That was not my final mission, here.

I dragged myself down the block to STD District Clinic 12, big as a Philly International gate, replete with vintage airport chairs, in rows; if you're up early enough to get a seat, you watch Jenny Jones.

I bided my time calling Andy to tell him I was driving to Mexico, and got a machine. Ricky bid me luck and told me he wished he could come along. It would be like this movie he'd just seen, he said, about two positive guys who go on a road trip. "The living end," he said. "It would be just like the living end." I knew he was trying to say something. I wanted to ask him how Paul was but I couldn't hear it yet. I stepped into the blizzard to chain-smoke Lucky Strikes, heard the mentholated women by the subway grill hiss, Kids just come here to find out they're gonna die. Number 88, ready to board? The social worker asked a million questions and I lied to every one. She gave me a toll-free number to call for results, and a code.

"Give it two weeks," she said. "Ninety-nine percent of all cases are detected in three months. That's when you should form antibodies," she clarified, jovially. I couldn't look up to see her face, but her voice ran up and down the octaves, edgy and unmodulated, like she'd seen too much go wrong.

"Oh. Three months." I hated to count back. "December, November, October. Only a little of September. Cool. I think. Thanks."

She handed me a bushel of condoms and told me to take care. That's when I nearly looked her in the eyes. I saw her lips, chapped, the pink stick awry on one cheek, and said to them:

"Trust me. I will."

On the way out I took a roll of Mr. Yuk stickers from the poison control desk. Two more weeks and then I'd know: Keep going south, or stop.

I stopped at an empty White Castle on the chill walk home for gristle on a biscuit. Blinding ice crystals had replaced all the leaves. Having acquired a bright red boot warning on Lombard, I'd parked for the last month on abandoned Mole, where even meter maids fear to tread. Planning to pull it around, I noticed my car was now officially part of the neighborhood; it was missing a window and someone had taken a shit on the emergency brake. Must have been recent, since it hadn't frozen over. Lucky for me, I had an array of high-powered bleaches from the stripping service in the hatchback.

Jockstraps make good rags. As soon as I got home from the clinic, I turned on public TV, on a whim, straight to a documentary of teens who had HIV. By the airing, one boy was already dead.

My medical pictures were a mad nostalgia that couldn't correspond with anything outside of themselves. My life was moving on. They had no choice but to either tag along or stay behind. Acting as Robin Hood, I donated certain pediatric clippings to the Art Institute, returned Herbert and Lois to pasture, and offered my crack to the tallest street girl I could find. I stuck Mr. Yuks on the navels of my reproduced boys, like tattoos: Danger! Poison! Do Not Touch! The only things left behind were my mattress, my TV, my projects, and tracings: Sicilian boys inextricably wedged between a cupboard and the fridge. Right in front, ominous traffic cops were stealing up to my pockmarked, shattered Sunbird. The snow was letting up. It seemed like a good time to go.

Philadelphia's luster shone behind me, the icy Schuylkill gleaming in the clear cold sun. A billboard for a gentleman's club read, *Leaving so soon? The time of your life is four miles back.* I didn't look back until I got on the turnpike at Valley Forge. I had to pull into the first rest stop. The bitter wind swirling through the broken glass made my eyes hurt. The time of my life was so many miles away.

Fugitive Emissions

Back in the cage, my father has left a nasty surprise, a combination lock circling through the old Master. Taped to the back is a series of tiny numbers, in his handwriting: 12011201220110022020202212120. Dad must be the only person on earth who can't remember a three-digit combination but can translate a trinary code in his head. I spend six hours gouging my fingernails and learning encryption techniques at my favorite old library before I finally crack the code: one-six-two. If the numbers had been any bigger, he'd have had to make them microscopic. When the lock gives, I realize how much we both love her, to go through all that effort to protect her soul.

Like a cat burglar, I steal Mom out of storage. Only some. He won't notice she's gone. She rides shotgun in a plastic bag on the passenger seat, like a drug.

The next morning, my sheets are all wet. My boxers are soaked, my pillow's a vapor. Words singe my shoulder: my name voiced aloud. Who out there's hissing this name from the living, you should say Mitch, Jeremy, Kevin, do you know my real name? No one knows my real name here—Eye, wake up, Eye, wake up, Ivan, wake up.

Cold sun shafts through the windows, I'm back in Milwaukee, the spare bed in Dad's study. The family that lives here now offered me shelter for as long as I need. Only Ichi, Dad's post-doc, speaks English. They smile a lot. When I get into Mexico, vans will stop chasing me. They can tell I'm anxious to leave.

Truth, says the stranger, *is stranger than fiction.* Of course I'm convinced she is speaking of me. A weary old man sits beside me, unblinking, bored sick and smacking Saltines. The red pleather diner booth sticks to my thighs. Now we're somewhere in Texas. A copper just nailed me for speeding, no less. My chicken-fried steak bristles up to Hank Williams, put another quarter in and let that sucker play. Could be a full moon and a lonely wolf's howl, a cub who is hungry or just wants to game. Knocking eggs over easy straight from the buffet, this lady's come down from I guess Corpus Christi. *Truth's stranger than fiction,* she said that today.

I've seen the Mayor everywhere, tall and heavy. In strip malls, diners, motel lobbies. The rib place in East St. Louis. The lonely bridge in Tulsa. The gas station in Galveston. And I have seen the staring people. They stand and watch as I pass. At the Wal–Mart in the Ozarks, a pregnant girl looked at me through a polyester smock display like she'd spotted a man from another planet. She picked out a hideous pastel floral with some defiance, as if challenging me: you think you got problems? I got to wear this, and don't that just beat all?

I want to say that *rain streamed in veins up the window as the train descended underground* and *the sky wept the whole way* and *the rims shrieked for me and the rails screamed in Camden.* In Elizabethtown, the laden front swept to the ground, its cold misery begging for pathos.

Fuck you, Eye, the clouds don't cry for you and you alone.

Mom and I go through the border gate at Brownsville. Before the shantytowns in hazy twilight, three fluorescent hours spent negotiating Mexican car insurance. Mom's Spanish is better than mine, and she's a good flirt, but it still takes two hundred dollars and the whole afternoon. The air is different almost immediately, the exotic incense of trash bonfires. We drive on empty tanks through dusty clapboard towns, splurge on a motel with a hot tub the first night. The morning sun through the wood lattice jacuzzi roof is as strong and complicated as love. We come from the sun and I want to go back. That afternoon we set a tent by the Gulf, a dune on the beach in the non-existent town of Tepeguajes. It's right on the Tropic of Cancer. No one lives there but seagulls, gray hawks, and butterflies in a forsaken cemetery on a bluff. Daggerwings and sprites skip over dangling crosses and crumbling headstones, flutter into a blue thatch of peonies. The waves are wide and slow, relentlessly silk-screening the sand, imprinting the land with their flow. I braid my hair with a bundle of small rubber bands and pad to the edge of the Gulf, to piss.

At dusk the sand has grown cold underfoot.

I'm the only person for miles. There hasn't been any other traffic all day. Unless you count the seagulls.

The next day, along the score of suspension bridges to Tampico, my gas station shrimp disagree with me violently. I unroll the window and vomit into the black, blinkered gulf until I'm completely empty inside. My Pontiac smells like I remember it. She helps me make ramen noodles in a pension we take for the night. I want to find that place in my mind, the jungle's edge where we can live, just Mom and me and our navy dome tent under the snaking vines of wild hibiscus. I learn Spanish from being lost. In San Luis Obispo I buy a bottle of brandy (*El sabor de la noche!* The flavor of the night!), nursing it in empty marble halls while she sleeps. Our grand hotel is a void, dispossessed. Housekeepers sleepily sweep halls for themselves, their broom strokes echoing, eerily, like fingernails against stone, the frenetic scratching of someone who's been buried alive.

We decide to go west, toward our destination, dust and road.

In Pátzcuaro, in the western central highlands, the elevation makes for cold nights. We buy three soft wool ponchos to wrap ourselves. The townspeople dress in four or five layers. As it gets progressively warmer during midday, up to 80 degrees, they strip down to T-shirts, and then bundle up again at sunset. They are always taking something off or putting something on. The streets are steep, leading up a hill to Our Lady of Good Health. From the old colonial church, you can look out at the descent of rust-red shingles, a testament to invention that is almost an optical illusion, a real-life Escher.

I buy Mom some Mexican chocolate, thin crispy medallions tightly stacked in a pink paper sack. She shares with me. They are as thin and airy as the breeze off the nearby lake, where the Purepecha kings would frolic and fish. She tells me the old myths that claim Janitzio, a tiny lake island, is the door of the sky where the natives descended. These days Janitzio is ringed by black sludge from the oil of motorized boats that take tourists around, but indigenous folk on the small island hillock still use cowhide canoes and butterfly netting when they dredge for whitefish. On the hard-pebbled shoals, men hack flesh into pieces, fling them onto makeshift stone braziers.

I carry Mom up the cobblestoned hill from our campground to the square, the Plaza Vasco de Quiroga. We learn from our campground owner that the celebrations for the Day of the Dead are incomparable, and in early November the town is besotted with orange marigolds, the Aztec flower for remembering the dead. Every year the fishing boats on Janitzio carry a procession of relatives who honor the entombed with offerings of flowers and *pan de muerte,* the bread of death. He gives us the recipe: it calls for orange peel and anise. Unfortunately, we're two months late. Today is market day, and the blackberries are plump and wet. We buy two paper bags worth and share them with three small children. I take color pictures of the red juice dripping from their happy mouths.

And once again, after this calm break, we cross the lonely mountains and into the atmosphere. Away from the lakes, the air becomes arid and crepuscular. The mountains are dry and brown and so remote that not even helicopters fly overhead, spraying their poison over papaverous hillsides. Every ten miles we stop to pour water into the radiator. After three days of desolate endless ridge I know no one can find me anymore.

"I feel safe," I tell Mom. Nothing can live here but scrub brush, and even that looks sick and parched.

I don't, Mom answers, staring out the double plastic of her bag and her window. *We need to keep going west. You could die here in the Sierra Madre and no one would ever know.*

"Isn't that the point?"

What's wrong with you? I can see her make a face as she regards me, then looks back to the sky, puts on her shades. I am driving us into the sun. *How are we on gas?*

"Quarter of a tank." I imagine touching her thigh, cool and plump. "We'll be okay, remember? We've got each other."

Shit, she says, *I feel like dirt.*

I'm glad we can talk to each other like adults. I feel closer to her than I have in years.

And gradually, in the lavender twilight, we begin to descend. The long plateau gives way to switchbacks and horseshoe curves, and my tires squeal pathetically. The needle's on empty but we can take it in neutral. Dirt becomes soil and bare hills are now verdant, emerald vines with long fat leaves. The air is thick and wet.

Can you smell it? She asks me, excited now. *I think I can smell the ocean.*

I know that's where she wants to go. I'm not ready yet. "Look!" I respond. "Can you see it? The green and white?"

I see her craning her neck to my side: *The Pacific?*

"Not quite. But I think there's a Pemex station two or three miles down." And there was, and past that, ten miles of hilly rain forest kissed by the coast, and just beyond, the deep black dusk of the sea.

We splurge for a cheap hostel bungalow in Playa Azul. We are so tired we don't bother to move our twin beds closer. The next morning, Mom asks for flour and oranges and anise seed and I walk around town to find the ingredients. I also buy tiny cookies, galletitas, as a treat.

Thanks, she says on my triumphal return. *If you want to go to the beach, just go. Have fun. I am just going to relax in here. Later we can bake some bread.*

I cruise up and down the shore, partly for the exercise and for the cool feel of the sand, the grit that turns to sludge beneath wet feet. The coast is an endless, sunbaked quagmire, which keeps me moving, north and south alongside, all day long.

I talk to strangers:

An older kid, maybe twenty-five, at the hostel. He's bald—shaved clean—but a blond goatee slides off his shin like angel hair. He sprained his ankle walking down the beach all day; or it was the tai chi, he doesn't know for sure. He's trying to get a job here, and get crutches. He's from somewhere in Brooklyn and commands the communal TV, which makes me suspect he's just faking his injury to watch his favorite shows.

A younger kid, maybe seventeen, who's from Seattle and here with his extended family—his cousins, grandparents, his maniacal mom, who's good-looking in that deep dark tan, bottle-blonde, aerobicized way. He asks me about bodysurfing. He's seen me get dragged into the sand. I teach him my technique; you have to tread and wait for cresting waves to come, then kick so you're horizontal and duck your head and stroke as if you're part of them. If you imitate the ocean's thrust, a good wave can take you all the way to shore. Then I look up from his two-tone Pumas. Two taut thighs. There is only darkness where they meet. His grin's punctuated by rubber bands that circum-navigate his gum line. He's sturdy, like a soccer player. The first time he sees me, water jetting from my nostrils as I struggle up the beach toward him, he smiles so big his rubber bands almost pop loose.

Two kids: a shy, brown-haired boy, fourteen; and his friend, a fifteen-year old girl, smiley and chunky, a Playa Azul native. The boy is originally from Chicago. He is short, maybe 5′3′′, pale and skinny. His pale eyes are the blue dawn of his swim trunks, almost transparent in equatorial sunlight. They lead me into a quarry where tiny silver fish flock. Their quick darting defies laws that my father knows. The girl is interested in me, but I throw her off by acting like a big brother. When she tells me about her twenty-year-old boyfriend, I say, "If you were my sister, I'd be worried about you, because guys are always out for sex." The girl says, "I'm a virgin. I'm not even attracted to him. He's ugly. He gives me stuff." I want her to leave so I can consume her friend. If I concentrate hard enough I know I can make his suit disappear, but she is distracting me. We talk about surfing. The boy does not surf. The outline of his cock makes a thin shadow in his shorts. When the girl realizes she's not my quarry, they leave me; he trails after her, apologetically. He does not come back. I stick my hand in the warm shallow water and the glossy fish disperse.

On the beach of an Americanized resort, a boy, maybe twelve, is with a much younger brother and two older sisters. "Can someone bury me in the sand?" he shouts loudly. "Anyone? Please you guys," he implores his wading siblings. "Please?" I take him up on the offer, ask them if it's okay. His sisters couldn't care less. Like a seal pup, he is hairless and wriggles. He throws sand over his crotch so I don't have to touch him. As I consolidate small stones over his stomach, a woman comes over.

"What are you doing?" she asks, shadowing me from the sun.

"I'm burying this kid in sand. He asked to be."

"Do his parents know what you're doing?"

"No, they're not even here. I asked his sisters. It's fine with them."

"You better stop. I don't want you to get in *any kind of serious trouble*," she says menacingly, and pads back to her perch, glaring back over her shoulder. She has two small girls with her.

"The fun police," the boy cracks. I'm trembling again and sit down, deflated, a kite torn by a power line.

"What is she even talking about?" I ask him.

"Stranger danger," he shrugs. "It's OK, I'll just bury myself."

Nearer the street, a sixty-year-old curly-haired New Bohemian from Nebraska gives me a Salem 100. She seems anxious to talk as the sun hides behind stray clouds. We talk about her son, who lives here and has married an Azulia, and her own incredulity upon arriving in Acapulco. "It took me two weeks to believe I was here! I've wanted to come here since I was a little girl! I just wish I could swim at the resort in Acapulco. Their beach is contaminated this week." She drove her RV for three weeks to make it. We discuss her suggestions for a drink: "Duke's, though I'm not sure who's singing tonight." Duke's is a beach bar, where Toltec sacrifice reenactments are staged for American tourists on the hour, where the bartender simply pockets the leftover change from my Pacifica. I like the frizzy, grizzled woman. She seems lonely, and happy.

A thirteen-year-old plays chess on the tables above the public beach. I buy a cactus salad across the street and return, bid for the next game. Homeless, toothless old men and women cohabit with the chess players and the bike cops. Under the picnic grove–style roof, the salty wind is tempered by wafts of urine. I ask the boy where he's from—Philly, it turns out. We share the joke: "Don't talk to anyone—" I say, "—Unless you want to get shot," adds the boy. He moved here three weeks ago with his parents; his dad's on assignment, whatever that means. He has smooth legs, short curly hair, glasses, a Math Champion T-shirt, and boy-scout-length tan shorts. A pimple is forming along one of the wings of his freckled nose. He asks where I'm staying, says, "I stayed in a hostel in Sacramento once. I didn't like it." What did he think of Sacramento? "It kind of sucked," he says, and checkmates me in sixteen moves. I'm distracted and outclassed and play too aggressively. He collects his chess pieces, seals them in a plastic bag, and rides off on his bike.

A nuclear American family occupies a square in the sand near what seems like the gay beach: a mom, a dad, a boy, a girl, the first half graying, the second half in full bloom. I ask them for the time. The dad says it's ten to six. I say thanks and almost walk off, but the son, who'd been supine on his stomach, gets up. His hard-on plows up his red trunks, and he half-lackadaisically, half-frantically tries to cover up with an unbuttoned button-down. Self-consciously needing a reason to stare, I fish for a smoke and ask if they have a light. Tracking the son's awkward movements, I pirouette like a Rittenhouse pigeon. "No," says the father, firmly. Some nearby German men in bikinis grin at me while I stand and chart the boy's fumbling: his dick up against his stomach, then straight out, tenting his suit, and finally, uncomfortably stretched down as he walks, bowlegged, to the sidewalk. He's about my age.

An old Japanese tourist walking down the pier with his wife offers me his lighter. I sit on a bench and smoke and watch the boy lace his shoes and button his shirt. As the family walks to the intersection of Morelia and Guerrero, I tag along. They wait for two lights to change. A white stretch limousine rolls past us, and the father explodes.

"Is there a reason why you're following us?" he demands in a voice that has nothing to do with the sun or the sky or the morning glories that stretch across stucco.

"Wha—?" I squint, caught slightly off guard, like the boys I like to look at, I'm supposing. "No . . . I'm just lost. I walked up and down the beach today and I'm just trying to find my way back home."

"Well, you won't find it from us," slams the dad. The light changes from a red wand to a pale silhouette, legs akimbo. And the family runs off to their fancy hotel, or wherever. I feel like I just got kicked in the balls.

A Mexican girl bums a smoke from me in exchange for another light. I stumble down the boardwalk and watch the boys boogieboard until the sun's flames fizzle into the water.

Back at the hostel, the owner's wife greets me. "Where you from?" she asks. "How long you staying?"

I tell her Wisconsin, and I really don't know. Maybe a week, maybe more.

"Wisconsin?" she says. "Up north, right? We haven't had a guest from Wisconsin in quite a while. Quite a while."

How long, I wonder. She seems to read my mind.

"Almost twenty years," she says. "Wonderful people. I still remember their names. We have a picture of them," she says. "Have you looked at our photos? Come look."

I follow her over clay tiles glazed with white birds with blue eyes and terracotta beaks. She turns on the lights in the common room (the TV-watchers groan) and points to the bulletin board. In the middle is a woman with freckles and wavy red hair, her arm around a man with a Jewish afro and thick red beard and soaked button-down, holding a screaming wet toddler.

"Nadia, Shlomo, and Ivan," she says proudly.

"Nadia, Shlomo, and Ivan," I whisper after her. We've all been here all along.

"Those are my parents," I tell her in Spanish. I don't want anyone else to know. "My name is Ivan but they call me Eye."

"No," she says, disbelieving. "No! But you do look like him," she smiles. "Welcome back," she says, also in Spanish. "I'm Estrella. You know, you're the reason we drained the pool. It is still empty today. Too much worry, and the sea is so close. Three times you jumped in! Three times! And each time your poor father jumped in to save you with all his clothes on." She laughs, shaking her head at the memory. "The last time you turned blue and he had to give you breath. And now look at you. Almost a man! Tell me, how are your parents?"

"My dad is okay. He's in Germany. I brought her with me. Nadia. She's in my room. I'll go get her."

Estrella is horrified when I show her Mom, but Mom's really happy to see her, I can tell. "My God," she says, crossing herself. "What happened?"

"She was studying ruins in Chiapas. She got really sick and had to leave. No one knows exactly what happened." My Spanish isn't good enough to explain any further. The docs seemed to think she'd consumed corn laden with DDT and warfarin, but I still think she was cursed by an angry Toltec mummy. "She was hospitalized. She was allergic to the medicine. This is part of what's left of her. She wanted to come back here." The tears come hot and salty, like the water in the quarry. I turn away and whisper. "She wants her ashes to fly over the Pacific like your white butterflies. It's what she's telling me."

"I am so sorry," she says, wiping her eyes. "She was so alive, you know." She pulls a pin out of the corkboard and hands me the fading Kodachrome. I try to politely decline. "Take it," she orders. "You must take it, you must. Stay as long as you need. Do what you must. Do what your mother wants."

Back in our room, I unclip the metal screen door, duck past whistling hinges into luminous cool, the locust buzz. Sounds like wolves are making love, or mourning the migrating monarchs, gone north to Carlsbad, or the Sonora. Soon I may follow them. The latch clicks shut behind me.

It is too easy to escape, and then again too hard. I cannot leave them behind. I cannot leave her fully, yet I have to leave her here, this part of her I have to jettison. Overhead, the waning moon reminds me: soon. When it disappears again, before it renews. All those light-years off and all that time long gone now. All those towns that drifted slowly by.

A corner of the building peels away, the straw and mud. I walk around the kitchen windows to the broken kiva, sit where flatbread used to bake and smell propane. Carlos is the owners' son, so it's good shit, homegrown. Deep breathing, eight good hits, then hyperventilate. Thoughts are dandelion dendrites, panic spores. Words slur into axions. Still, there are certain things to know for sure:

I'll be twenty-one soon.

My name is Ivan but they call me Eye.

Eye is the same backwards and forwards.

Mom's in a bag on the bed.

My brain is a ball of well-wound rubber bands, bouncing around the following: it's four thousand miles from Jersey, give or take. Also, you can see a storm miles away here, when it's perfectly sunny. Walking showers, they're called. Everyone's favorite song is "Soy la Basurita," meaning *I am the little piece of trash.*

As the broom of the gods, the wind of the night, sweeps the dust from the sky, I can sense what I miss: her smile, showing small even teeth, an inner lip's wet sunset. Her angular cheeks, denting a lumpy pillow, as she jawbones her way through uneasy dreams.

Now the door clicks shut, the cherry's gone. It flickers out in the dark red dust. I flick off the lights, set the roach on a thick wooden windowsill, kick off new moccasins. The stone floor is cold on my soles. I sit on the ancient swivel-chair to a muffled screech of iron, inflame a votive candle on the blue Formica table. I run a hand along its ridged chrome siding, stare at Mary, supplicant.

She looks like Mom, when I was little, playing Sorry!

I'm sick of missing being little.

Light a match, burn a fingertip a bit, to flinch.

Over tostadas tonight at the Rancho de la Playa, I fell in love with a busboy, redheaded Leandro, from the mountains.

She wants to be scattered in the ocean. She wants to set sail. She's possessed. Inside the bag, her spirit, pregnant, pressing. On the counter, the anise, the orange, the flour. Tomorrow I will become a man.

And so tonight, when I'm still little Eye, it is only safe to remember boyhood, to imagine Leandro's freckled shoulders upholding denim straps, naked arms milking the afternoon's long shadows.

I look to the other bed, the bulging baggie twisted into knots. She used to tell those stories of me as a toddler, tinkering too close to the water's edge, tumbling into pools before I could swim. *Your father saved you three times,* she would say, *corduroys, fountain pens, wallet, and all.* I feel protectiveness welling inside me, like I'd do just that. I'm still here, after all, and can hardly recall what the surface looked like from the bottom, bubbling with Dad's resolve.

Instead what I remember is the song he would sing on long road trips to the Badlands, to pick her up from a dig. Absent-minded, almost silent, he'd breathe his lullaby's life into the dry, quiet nights.

Go to sleep, my weary hobo. Let the towns drift slowly by. Can't you hear the steel rims humming? That's the hobo's lullaby.

Soon, I'll blow Mary out, close my lids to the flame's inlaid turquoise, stumble through the other room. Lift her nightshirt. Fasten lips around her navel, the tie in the plastic, like it's a third nipple. My nose will skim skin, the nape of her neck, thin fuzz of her mustache, and allow me a last glimpse of my first kiss: a maple leaf's spiral, a football, a nine-year-old boy, how it all began.

In packs, in some unconscious phalanx, the boys converge for waves. They float, supine, faces angled toward Samoa. Their asses gleam, half in canvas, beaded with saltwater, sleek with dusk. I watch them from the pier. The younger set, eight to twelve, stay near the shore. They fling their boards against the skim and race to leap on them. Waves fling them into somersaults, into the sea. The older set, sixteen to fifty-five, stay fifty yards offshore, bobbing steady until they feel whatever tidal pull precedes a big kahuna. They'll ride it in if it holds up. A spackling of guys play both these roles. They are the most interesting.

I borrow a shortboard that washed up, long ago, onshore. (The hostel has a collection of decaying sea devices.) I walk to the edge of the promontory, gulp, and vault into blackness as night falls. I am new at this, and other young men sense it. I lose my board on the back of a foaming crest. A boy saves it for me wordlessly. Like the adolescents, I bob between the shallows and the deep.

The ocean swells. Forty boys and forty boards float forward in silent unison. I am one of them.